WHY DID A NUMBER OF PREVIOUSLY DOCILE ELEPHANTS ATTEMPT TO KILL THEIR TRAINERS?

WHAT CAUSED MILLIONS OF CROWS TO DIVEBOMB A SMALL CALIFORNIA TOWN?

WHY DID TOTALLY CONTENTED DOGS SUDDENLY TURN ON THEIR OWNERS?

WHAT DROVE WAVE AFTER WAVE OF HAMMERHEAD SHARKS TO ATTACK BATHERS IN THE WATERS AROUND CORPUS CHRISTI, TEXAS?

These are just a few of the bizarre and frightening events which are occurring with greater and greater regularity. Devastating invasions by ants, bees, locusts, and gnats, unexpected attacks by birds, fish, and animals are taking place almost daily. What is behind these sweeping changes in the behavior of the creatures of the Earth?

STORM ON THE SUN offers startling answers to these questions, providing all the latest information on solar research, and pointing up some of the amazing developments which await us in the near future.

Mystic Books from SIGNET

☐ **ASTROLOGY: The Space Age Science by Joseph F. Goodavage.** A well-documented case for the science of astrology, the study of how the cosmic power of the stars affects man's life. (#Y6780—$1.25)

☐ **MAGIC: Science of the Future by Joseph F. Goodavage.** This book reveals the long-suppressed facts about the most basic force in the cosmos—psionics, the Universal Field of Life. (#W7081—$1.50)

☐ **SELF MASTERY THROUGH SELF HYPNOSIS by Dr. Roger Bernhardt and David Martin.** This breakthrough book shows you how to use hypnosis to improve your ability and performance in every area of your life with this fully tested, dramatically effective, 30-seconds-a-day method. (#J8352—$1.95)*

☐ **KATHRYN KUHLMAN: The Woman Who Believes in Miracles by Allen Spraggett.** In this inspiring story of the greatest faith healer since Biblical times, Allen Spraggett gives a number of indisputable case histories of the cures that Kathryn Kuhlman has effected. (#W8529—$1.50)*

☐ **NEW WORLDS OF THE UNEXPLAINED by Allen Spraggett.** The astonishing, true-life experiences of people who have crossed over that invisible boundary into the unknown. . . . (#W6876—$1.50)

*Price slightly higher in Canada.

If you wish to order any of these titles, please use the coupon in the back of this book.

STORM on the Sun

by
Joseph F. Goodavage

A SIGNET BOOK
NEW AMERICAN LIBRARY
TIMES MIRROR

NAL BOOKS ARE ALSO AVAILABLE AT DISCOUNTS IN BULK
QUANTITY FOR INDUSTRIAL OR SALES-PROMOTIONAL USE.
FOR DETAILS, WRITE TO PREMIUM MARKETING DIVISION,
NEW AMERICAN LIBRARY, INC., 1301 AVENUE OF THE
AMERICAS, NEW YORK, NEW YORK 10019.

Copyright © 1979 by Joseph F. Goodavage

All rights reserved

SIGNET TRADEMARK REG. U.S. PAT. OFF. AND FOREIGN COUNTRIES
REGISTERED TRADEMARK—MARCA REGISTRADA
HECHO EN CHICAGO, U.S.A.

SIGNET, SIGNET CLASSICS, MENTOR, PLUME and MERIDIAN BOOKS
are published by The New American Library, Inc.,
1301 Avenue of the Americas, New York, New York 10019

FIRST SIGNET PRINTING, APRIL, 1979

1 2 3 4 5 6 7 8 9

PRINTED IN THE UNITED STATES OF AMERICA

DEDICATION

For my brothers, Edward, Vincent, and William, for their patience, generosity, and love through many years—even when *they* needed it most.

Acknowledgments

My thanks to Dr. John Gribbon for his help in pointing out the direction even when I didn't accept his views, to my daughter Diana for changing hers, and to Evelyn Goodavage for her invaluable assistance with an unusual manuscript. I'm also deeply grateful to Richard Preble for his help, moral support, and friendship—but mainly for his faith.

... the inertia of the human mind and its resistance to innovation are most clearly demonstrated not, as one might expect, by the ignorant mass—which is easily swayed once its imagination is caught—but by professionals with a vested interest in tradition and in the monopoly of learning. Innovation is a twofold threat to academic mediocrities; it endangers their oracular authority, and it evokes the deeper fear that their whole laboriously constructed intellectual edifice may collapse.

—ARTHUR KOESTLER, *The Sleepwalkers*

Contents

Introduction		1
Chapter 1	The Star	5
Chapter 2	Earthquakes, UFOs, and Ghosts	14
Chapter 3	Supergiants and the Holy Solar Corona	31
Chapter 4	Electromagnetic Pollution: The Wild Kingdom on a Rampage	48
Chapter 5	Electromagnetic Fields of Life	62
Chapter 6	Tesla Electrifies the Earth	79
Chapter 7	Velikovsky: Destroyer of Worlds	99
Chapter 8	Scientists in Collusion	122
Chapter 9	Who Goes There?	141
Chapter 10	Cosmic Cycles, Climate, and World Civilization	162
Chapter 11	The Seven Faces of God	179

STORM
on the Sun

Introduction

There are obviously questions for which there are no answers, and neither logic, metaphor, nor emotion will have an impact on certain states of mind. There is a story of Haroun Mohammed el Rashid, who once tried to spark the fire of logic that would help illuminate the mind of a merchant named Nadji Sri Lanka. Unfortunately, logic had no effect whatever on Nadji's mind, which was greedy and materialistic.

Rashid, however, patiently tried to illustrate his point by allegory. He told Nadji the story of a man who, on a warm spring morning, fell asleep in the shade of a great tree and dreamed that he was a wondrously large, beautiful, and colorful butterfly. And when the man finally awoke he could not truly remember if he was a man who had dreamed he was a butterfly or a butterfly dreaming it was a man.

The true state of our individual consciousness is usually on a physical level—one of materialistic want or need. Seldom do we consider the possibility that we are doing all the things we do *not* from autonomous free choice but in conformance with a large overall field, an intangible matrix of pure energy somewhat similar to a magnetic field extending through space in three dimensions.

The immense power of a field that existed in four, five, or more dimensions and kept everything from atoms to galaxies "going" just as a perfect machine, an infinitely intelligent machine, might function, may be as far beyond human comprehension as the concept of a Supreme Creator or anthropomorphic God.

There is one enormous power source that offers certain clues to such exotic questions—the Sun. As H.

Introduction

...sberg, director of climatology of the United ...es Weather Bureau, said, "One reliable observation is worth a thousand models and a million speculations."

Our local star, the one object we take most for granted, has certain mysterious functions, as John H. Nelson notes in his book, *The Occult Sun* (New York: Harper & Row, 1977). While working for RCA, Inc., astronomer Nelson discovered a system of predicting sunspots and solar flares according to the positions of the planets. He used this system to predict radio weather for RCA for nearly thirty years. His record of accuracy: 93 percent.

The Sun has many cycles and "beats"; my observation is that its functions conform to every definition of a living entity. It generates and radiates a force of enormous strength and subtlety—one that can only be detected indirectly. Since this energy transcends the known electromagnetic spectrum, we can call it *the superspectrum*. The influence of this *superspectrum* is reflected in the cycles of world history, in wars, economic cycles, and the seemingly improbable cycles of all living things.

The Sun is oscillating, parts of its surface rising and falling between 700 to 1,400 miles every five minutes. Its equatorial "girdle" speeds up and slows down for no apparent reason. At the same time, acoustic waves vibrate throughout the Sun's 864,000-mile diameter every hour or two. Fortunately, we can't hear it, but the Sun actually "rings" like a colossal bell. Our star flickers and oscillates and undoubtedly reacts in thousands of unknown ways.

According to the currently accepted scientific model, the Sun's interior is so dense that radiation received on Earth today was produced at the star's core several millions of years ago. According to solar physicists, each photon released by the fusion of hydrogen into helium emits a particle that travels a short distance and is absorbed by another subatomic particle. Thus do photons struggle in a maze-like jigsaw fashion against the stupendous pull of the mightiest

Introduction

gravitational force within trillions and trillions of miles of space.

Something is terribly wrong with our most basic conceptions about what is going on inside the Sun. According to the current theoretical view, these particles—photons, gamma rays, X-rays, and very long radio waves—struggle against the enormous pull of solar gravity for years. Through some as-yet-mysterious "mechanism" they burst forth, instantly achieving escape velocity (i.e., light speed, 186,200 mps). But how, and at what point? Without this miracle, there could be no radiation. The Sun wouldn't shine. It would, in theory, be a black hole.

Almost everything we nonphysicists know about the theory of relativity is that nothing can go faster than light. This is offensive to some people and absolutely enrages others, who know perfectly well that the Starship *Enterprise* flashes around the Galaxy at multiple-multiple light speeds (and always encounters intelligent, humanoid, oxygen-breathing, English-speaking aliens).

The cliché "Truth is stranger than fiction" holds water. In 1864 only crackpots and addlepated nonagenarians believed in Plato's accounts of the destroyed continent of Atlantis or Homer's description of Troy. Heinrich Schleimann, however, took Homer seriously, ignored those who ridiculed and hounded him, and discovered the lost city of Troy exactly where Homer had described its location. Heinrich Schleimann is now recognized as one of the greatest archaeologists who ever lived.

The Epic of Gilgamesh told the story of Creation 2,000 years before the writers of the Bible got around to writing Genesis. The Epic told of great "Sons of heaven who arrived from the skies amid thunder, smoke, and fire." Similar creatures, called "Angels" from heaven forewarned Lot and his family about the coming destruction of Sodom and Gomorrah.

In 1971 a group of students constructed an ark exactly according to the instructions issued "by

Introduction

God"—including special clothing and shoes to insulate them. Those Old Testament specifications resulted in a strange kind of electrical transformer (which was destroyed).

The clues to many of the mysteries of science are, in retrospect, easy to find. And always dualistic. The model of the evolution of our planet, geologically, is one of very gradual change, no sudden catastrophes that could have interrupted history. On the other hand, tens of thousands of imperial mammoths, mastodons, and other temperate-to-tropical-zone animals are frozen in upright positions, many with fresh grasses, ferns, and flowers in their mouths and stomachs. Since it takes about eight hours to mist-freeze an already dead twenty-five-pound turkey, it is hard to imagine what sudden drop in temperature could cause a five-ton, hot-blooded living mammal to be frozen before it could take a single step.

At about the time Cortez and his Conquistadores were erasing the Aztec civilization, an already ancient copy of a map of the Earth as seen from directly over Cairo, Egypt, was in the possession of a Dutch seaman named Piri Reiss. The year was 1532, yet the map clearly showed the exact outline of the continent of Antarctica, which "had not yet been discovered."

Of the thousands of baffling mysteries whose sources can be traced back to ancient times, the most puzzling of all is that of our own origin and existence, of the Sun that provides all our life's energies, and the recent strange changes in the behavior of our great star.

The tantalizing leitmotif that links them all somehow concerns electricity, magnetism, and electromagnetic energy, the force of which we are all a part. The genesis of our legends, myths, and religions seems to be a clouded version of vastly advanced creatures—either "nonphysical" Beings of pure energy or an extraordinarily rarefied version of the known electromagnetic field—the *superspectrum*, the L-field or universal field of Life.

The only local source of such a *superspectrum* is the Sun.

CHAPTER 1

The Star

> Eliminate the impossible. Whatever remains, however improbable, must be true.
>
> SHERLOCK HOLMES

A simple fact, now common knowledge to every schoolchild, was the product of gigantic intellectual effort on the part of one of science's greatest figures, Galileo, who tried in vain to convince the Holy Inquisitors and Church Fathers that Copernicus's heliocentric theory was correct.

Today nearly everyone knows that the Earth is not only *not* the center of the Universe, but merely one of our star's planets spinning on its axis and revolving in an eccentric orbit around the Sun. Strangely enough the Sun now seems to be part of a mysterious *binary* star system. This fact alone may completely revolutionize most of the sciences and shatter our entire view of human history.

The visible half of this mysterious dual star system—our Sun—is but one of billions of brilliant lights among just one of millions of whirling galaxies—all still exploding apart at incredible speeds from the theoretical Big Bang at the birth of the Universe. "Our" star? It may be the other way around. The very cells and molecules of our body and brain are part of the Sun. We star-born creatures are now faced with the inescapable fact that our familiar, so taken-for-granted Sun is totally, profoundly unlike *anything* conceived by anyone during humanity's brief known history.

This makes mankind's real destiny unlike anything

our scientific beliefs have ever hinted at or prepared us for. Civilization may have other, utilitarian purposes that—at least in a clearly conscious way—we've been all but incapable of thinking about. Few cyberneticians or other scientists, for example, would dare suggest that the recent acceleration of scientific and technological progress could be the result of something other than human free choice. The facts, however, indicate that it may be the result of programming infinitely more delicate than anything we've yet dreamed of achieving with our own creations, the computers.

One of man's most persistent skills has been his historic tendency to wage war—to kill, maim, conquer, or destroy his own kind. Can such behavior be the free choice of the majority of people throughout all historical eras? Probably not. When one accumulates as much of the "proper" information as possible and fits the pieces together, the emerging picture does something rather strange to the psyche. The experience can be shattering, particularly among ardent adherents to any of the great movements—whether nationhood, political supremacy, racial superiority, or the only true hot-line to God. These movements, with all their many branches and facets, one suspects, may actually be part of a strange kind of "programming" of the human species, one that, if understood, may lead to an explanation and understanding of mankind's predisposition to warfare, destruction, and reconstruction.

We all know, of course, that no one *really* wants war, but we must defend ourselves, mustn't we? Vast rivers of wealth are used to purchase the best scientific and engineering brains to develop weapons capable of such widespread and hideous devastation that the mind staggers trying to fathom the labyrinthine irrationality of mass human behavior.

Something seems terribly wrong. Perhaps we're not responsible for the fact that all the great religions traditionally teach love and brotherhood—then lustily slaughter those who don't subscribe to their version of universal love and peace. Virtually every religion has made taboo most of the things we humans are, by our very natures, inclined to do. The "thou shalt nots" cover just about all our basic instincts.

We don't really seem to be masters of our own destiny at all.

A group of medical students, following the pioneering work of Dr. José Delgado (who implanted radio controls into the brains of animals), decided to amuse themselves by applying remote-control electrical stimulation of the sex-arousal centers in the brains of several pairs of rhesus monkeys. The experiment must have been great fun because increasing numbers of students just couldn't resist operating the switches that literally forced the monkeys to screw themselves almost to death.

Whichever way that strikes you and whatever your reaction, try—just for a second—to put yourself in the place of one of those monkeys.

ITEM: Man is also a bio-electromagnetic animal.

ITEM: Psionic engineers have demonstrated that long-range Electromagnetic control of the brain *without* wiring or instrumentation is possible.

Essentially, all electromagnetic activity originates on and in the Sun, which is, as far as we know, the only truly "living" thing in the solar system. All life processes, all motion and energy, are controlled by the Sun. Volcanic activity, weather, earthquakes, and all other activity within the entire retinue of planets, including, as we shall see, human (and nonhuman) feelings, and nearly every form of behavior, are but a reflection of the constant output of solar energy.

According to Dr. Edward R. Harrison of the University of Massachusetts, an ominous new element may be disturbing our local star, a dark companion, of equal mass to the Sun, that seems to be in a hyperbolic orbit—like that of a comet—taking about 10,000 years for a single revolution.

"This could bring it close enough," wrote science editor Walter Sullivan (*The New York Times*, November 14, 1977), "as Dr. Harrison believes it is now, to have an effect on the solar system—and perhaps influence climate on Earth.

"At the other end of its orbit it [the dark body] would come close to the 'sea' of comets believed to envelope the solar system at a great distance..."

Further studies and new discoveries suggest that solar radiations extend far beyond the known, detectable electromagnetic spectrum. There is, in fact, evidence of a *superspectrum*, which may help explain some of the recent bizarre activity of the Sun, of weather on Earth, and even of human consciousness. (To my "scientific" friends, please consider our *true* situation—a kind of surface "scum"—one of many thousands of kinds of Beings on the "paper-thin" surface of our star's third planet.

Our local star is neither inanimate nor an object. It may not be insensate. Perhaps it possesses unknown, even unknowable powers far beyond present human intellectual abilities. Solar scientists were recently baffled to discover that for mysterious reasons the Sun simply "went off the boil." Allowing for the limitations of our finest sensors, these scientists are increasingly sure that something could be terribly wrong with the Sun.

Is this due, as Dr. Harrison's belief might suggest, to the fact that it is co-orbiting an invisible companion of comparable mass at a distance about 1,000 times greater (1,000 A.U.'s or astronomical units) than that between the Earth and Sun? Possibly. If our local star *is* approaching perihelion (closest orbital passage) to a mysterious, unseen companion of great mass—perhaps a collapsed star or a black hole—after 10,000 years, we may yet discover clues to the disappearances of advanced ancient cultures during prehistoric catastrophes, ice ages, or other perturbations that wiped out all trace of those antediluvian civilizations. Or—we may have some clue to the origin of life on Earth.

Although such concepts may at first seem vague or abstract, in just about every sense, the world we know is profoundly abstract. Particle physicists cannot see an electron. By itself, it's unobservable; from a practical, objective viewpoint, therefore, it does not exist as an entity in itself. Only when it unites with other particles (electron + protron + neutron) does it come into being for us as an atom. Thus, the whole is born of its parts.

In the same way, the world we know and all its parts are substantially abstract. For example, any organized system, whether it's a television receiver, a novel, a song, a painting, or a living creature, is essentially abstract. Where were you, for example, when Alexander the Great led his conquering legions across the Asian continent more than 2,000 years ago? Every element of your future composition was *somewhere*, but events and conditions had not yet organized (or *been* organized) into the integral series of coherent systems that is now you.

Where was radio communication in 1850? It took the right combination of purposeful thoughts and actions to discover radio waves, to invent broadcasting and receiving sets, and then to develop them into a viable system of communication. It took the right combination of motivations and germ cells to produce each of us—*and to produce life itself*. Presumably, there was a time when no life at all existed on the Earth's barren, primordial surface.

According to evolutionists (currently at war with biblical creationists), amino acids and other chemical agents were floating around in millions of ammoniated pools when, with purely random zaps of electromagnetic lightning bolts, they were lashed into the very "soup of life" itself. From those ancient slimy pools, claim the evolutionists, emerged all life as we know it today.

During an interview with the foremost (or at least the best-known) exobiologist in the country, I inquired about the incredible complexity and balance of the terrestrial ecology. "Was that purely by chance, random, or accident?"

"Charles Darwin, 1859," he answered, referring, of course, to the great British naturalist's revolutionary work, *Origin of Species*.

"But what about form, plan, organization?" I persisted.

"Charles Darwin, 1859," he said.

"Then consciousness and intelligence are mere accidents, with neither plan nor reason?"

"Charles Darwin, 1859," replied the brilliant scientist.

By an odd coincidence, 1859 was the year the Swedish chemist and Nobel Prize winner Svante August Arrhenius was born. He claimed that space was filled with "spores of life" which continually drifted to all the planets, just as terrestrial plant seeds are carried by winds and take root on rocky, isolated islands. Arrhenius, who became the father of the Transpermian Theory, was regarded as being mildly eccentric, if not an outright crackpot.

But he had followers. By 1976, Dr. Fred Whipple, former director of the Smithsonian's Center for Astrophysics at Harvard, announced that 1974's comet Kohoutek, rather than being a scientific fiasco, was actually the best-observed comet in history. "I don't feel apologetic that it brightened by only a million times," he told the American Philosophical Society. Kohoutek, rather than being "the century's biggest fizzle," actually revealed "an array of organic molecules somewhat reminiscent of an elementary course in organic chemistry."

Dr. Whipple went on to suggest that the volatile materials necessary for life—oxygen, nitrogen, and other elements—could have been sprinkled on the Earth by comets. "In any case," he told his audience, "I can say confidently that a significant fraction of the atoms in your bodies came from comets."

By November, 1977, two distinguished British astronomers, Sir Fred Hoyle and Professor Chandra Wickramasinghe, postulated that the essential building blocks of life were not formed in the "primeval soup" of primitive Earth—the normally accepted theory, but rather in the core and tails of comets. "All life on Earth, therefore, could have come from outer space, and major epidemics like influenza and the plague may still be coming from there," these astronomers announced. Millions of years ago a comet could have crash-landed on Earth, bringing the primitive organisms from which all life has evolved.

By their own admission their theory has "profound biological, medical, and sociological implications. If life did start that way, invasions of Earth by *fresh* biological material from the debris of comets is likely still to be continuing, and could account for past epidemics and plagues which spread quickly round the world at a time when travel was painfully slow."

It would also mean that we may expect new epidemics to come in the same way. "A continual microbiological vigil of the stratosphere may well be necessary to eliminate the havoc which will ensue from extraterrestrial invasions of the future," the astronomers claimed. Such material could reach the Earth on clumps of debris from comets as the Earth swings across their tails.

As far back in history as there are records, observers saw the connection between comets and plagues. The Old Testament (First Book of Chronicles) related how King David hid on the threshing floor at Ornam when his terrified followers first saw a great comet. Its flaming tail stretched all the way across the sky and appeared to envelop the Earth. Before the comet reached its perihelion (closest approach to the Sun), a great plague broke out and a deadly disease killed more than 70,000 people.

The Black Plague of 1665 killed uncounted millions of people as it swept around the world. The deadly disease erupted immediately after the Earth had passed through the tail of a spectacular comet. The populations of cities, towns, and villages were decimated over and over again as the plague raced back and forth across land and sea.

The infamous Black Death of 1347, the worst epidemic of bubonic plague ever known, coincided with a brilliant comet seen throughout Europe, Asia, and the Nordic countries. A helpless humanity, cursed by the dreaded disease, "perished like millions of rats" trying to flee from the pestilence. Half the world's population died.

Five years before the first man set foot on the Moon, a group of astronomers at Britain's Cambridge Observatory discovered that microbe life actually existed on Venus. If the Britishers' discovery has been verified by Soviet or American space probes, it has yet to be announced.

It happened that microorganisms blown from the highest reaches of the Venusian atmosphere by the solar wind, attacked the gelatinous emulsion of exposed photographic plates used in their surveys of the heavens. The tiny organisms were traced to the soft rainwater that was drained from the rooftops of the observatory and used to wash the plates. The mystery was solved when the astronomers noticed a curious coincidence: the voracious microbes eating holes in their photographic plates appeared *only* after the plates were washed with rainwater when Venus was directly aligned (*in superior conjunction*) between the Earth and Sun!

You'll read here how solar cycles and extremely low frequency (ELF) electromagnetic fields from the Sun and Earth coincide with historical cycles, how one man succeeded in electrifying the entire Earth, and some of the most astonishing evidence that the Sun itself may be "programmed" by great Beings of pure energy, infinitely more superior to man than humans are to microbes.

As the supposedly highest form of life on this planet, Homo sapiens is peculiarly susceptible to the known radiations from the Sun, and, by huge holes in the solar corona, from the unseen, unfelt, undetected *superspectrum*.

Benjamin Franklin sincerely believed the Sun was not just alive and sentient but actually a god: "Pray only to your local deity," he taught his followers, "the Sun."

The great French Jesuit scientist, Pierre Teilhard de Chardin, was convinced that the entire human species is evolving in a somewhat different way—*psychically*.

Teilhard, a geologist, paleontologist, and discoverer of Pekin Man, noted that "the probable life of a phylum of average dimensions is reckoned in tens of millions of years." Long before the discovery that the earliest known humanoid was almost five million years old—with extrapolations of human existence dating back more than ten million years—de Chardin wrote, "Man now sees that the seeds of his ultimate dissolution are at the heart of his being. The *End of the Species* is in the marrow of our bones!"

He qualified this seemingly dismal forecast, explaining that he meant "The end of a 'thinking species': not disintegration and death, but a new break-through and a re-birth, this time outside Time and Space, through the very excess of unification and coreflexion."

It is this kind of metamorphosis that Arthur C. Clarke and Stanley Kubrick tried to convey in the film, *2001: A Space Odyssey*.

But Teilhard had an even greater evolutionary view. In *Mon Univers*, he foresaw the end of the world: ". . . forced together by the growth of a common power and the sense of a common travail, the men of the future will in some sort form a single consciousness and because, their initiation being completed, they will have measured the power of their associated minds, the immensity of the Universe and the narrowness of their prison, this consciousness will be truly adult, truly major."

If men are to become gods—with powers unimaginable to the human brain in its present state—there must be evidence that other gods—possibly from a remote galaxy or dimension—have created us in their own image.

There is such evidence. Many diverse cultures have similar legends, myths, and religions featuring seven mighty archangelic figures, with the central Being responsible for the creation of the Sun, Moon, and planets, the land, sea, animals—and man. Entities capable of such awesome power would have no difficulty controlling a relatively small star such as our Sun.

CHAPTER 2

Earthquakes, UFOs, and Ghosts

> If you do not expect it, you will not find the unexpected, for it is hard to find and difficult.
> HERACLITUS

Does the Sun help produce earthquakes? Without a doubt. If there were no soli-lunar planetary interaction (gravitational, electromagnetic, and other cosmic energies), the Earth's activities would stop functioning—there would be no weather, no volcanic activity, no water, no tides, no life—nothing.

Beyond its familiar electromagnetic spectrum, a more subtle and powerful energy pattern—a *superspectrum*—radiates from the Sun. This field envelops the solar system's planets and may be a mode of instantaneous communication—perhaps travel—to the most remote parts of the Universe or other dimensions. Our local star is indeed a great enigmatic body, a paranormal object insofar as the physical sciences are concerned. The Sun's role in human destiny is barely suspected, as John H. Nelson points out in his book *The Occult Sun* (New York: Harper & Row, 1977). For more than twenty-five years, astronomer Nelson predicted solar activity for RCA, Inc. (with 93 percent accuracy, by the way), according to the positions of the planets. He was called a "Weather Propagation Analyst," but was, in fact, a fine astrologer. Electromagnetic storms and solar flares disrupt the ionosphere and destroy short-wave radio communications; John Nelson was able to predict months in advance when the Sun would be acting up, so that RCA could shut down and save manpower, money, and energy.

Although most scientists are "against" astrology, ghosts, and (except for our present scientist/President Jimmy Carter) UFOs, there are thousands of established natural occurrences whose basic causes are complete riddles to the physical sciences. Nature, for example, has decreed that 96 girls are born for every 100 males. It hardly seems "coincidental" that the mortality rate among male infants is 4 percent higher than that among females.

Even more astonishing to geneticists and sociobiologists are the unexplainable ratios between single births and twins, triplets, and quadruplets: for every 86 single births there is one twin birth. For every 86 twin births there is one triplet birth, and for every 86 triplet births there is one quadruplet birth. Present evidence seems to indicate that there may be one quintuplet birth for every 86 sets of quadruplets. Multiplying each result by 86, we find that one set of triplets is born in each population group of approximately 7,000 people. And in each segment of about 600,000 people there is one set of quadruplets. It should, therefore, take almost 50 million people to produce one set of quintuplets, and a population of over four billion to produce one set of sextuplets!

Odd natural "coincidences" like this have been observed and recorded throughout history. Maverick researcher Charles Hoy Fort, author of *The Book of the Damned, Lo!, New Lands* and *Wild Talents*, enjoyed pricking the self-esteem of astronomers and other scientific authorities who explained away everything that wasn't in their textbooks as mass hysteria, mistaken identity, self-hypnosis, mirages—anything but the total mysteries many of them were. Observing the eternal procession of reports of lights and other strange sightings in the empty skies—the "rains" of fish, frogs, metal, blood, ice, "angel hair," worms, birds, and sundry improbable, unlikely, and "impossible" objects that fell from the upper regions of the atmosphere, Fort concluded: "I think we're property." And after he reported a long series of weird disappearances of some people, and the even stranger reappearances of others, often naked, hungry, amnesiac, and unable to speak any known language, Fort observed: "I think we're fished for."

He spent years poring over news reports, magazine articles, and science journals, collecting more than 40,000 documented cases of events the scientists of his day almost unanimously rejected. Fort was the pluperfect master of obtuse skepticism. Not only did he *not* believe any of the pronouncements of the scientists of his time, he also warned his readers to doubt his own rhetoric and "preposterous" conclusions. "One measures a circle, beginning anywhere," he said, indicating that everything in this or any other universe is related or connected in some way with every other thing, and that there is not much difference between an elephant and a fly, except in matters of degree. This was over sixty years before scientists concluded that all terrestrial life is based on the DNA molecule.

Fort devoted a large part of his time to researching ghostly lights seen in the sky, on land, and under the oceans of the world. Eyewitnesses for thousands of years have reported sightings of what we now generally refer to as UFOs, but in addition to these unidentified, often glowing flying objects, other strange lights have been seen in the sky before major earthquakes. At times the entire atmosphere in the vicinity of an impending quake glows brighter than two full moons. There are thousands of recorded instances of the sky glowing like sheet lightning, of auroral streamers, fireballs, beams, or columns of light that were seen as far as 200 miles from the site of various earthquakes. In the most devastating earthquake (in terms of hundreds of thousands of human lives lost), the massive upheaval in 1976 in Tangsham, China, the entire sky lit up *during* the quake. A Mexican seismologist, Dr. Cinna Lomnitz, happened to be there when the quake struck. "The sky was lit up like daylight," he reported, "bright enough to wake people up, thinking their room lights had been turned on."

Lightning and meteors had been reported at the site of volcanic eruptions and earthquakes long before the birth of the modern industrial civilization. Charles Fort collected thousands of cases, and cited the ancient explanations, which are only now recognized as being close to the truth. As Seneca told the Romans more than 2,200 years ago, *"The world would rather cling to a wrong idea than accept a new truth."*

Several of the most unacceptable ideas today seem to be that UFOs are some kind of spaceships from other worlds and that ghosts, poltergeists, strange hauntings, and apparitions exist independently of the observer. The final explanation may be much simpler, yet vastly more intriguing.

The low-level oscillation of the atmosphere during or preceding great seismic upheavals seems to result in the generation of extremely low frequency (ELF) electromagnetic fields that (a) not only cause electrical luminosity of the atmosphere but (b) also directly influence the brain by being in almost perfect synchronization with human brain wave activity.

Yet when the most sensitive instruments are located only a few inches from the brain (during encephalographic measurements), they cannot detect the presence of brain waves. According to Dr. Michael A. Persinger of Laurentian University's Psychophysiology Laboratory in Canada, the propagation of human psi phenomena across distances as vast as hundreds or even thousands of miles requires *trillions* of times more energy than the human brain is capable of producing.

"The energy required for those paranormal cases which do not primarily involve peculiarities in brain chemistry . . . does not originate in the organism," he reported in "Geophysical Models for Parapsychological Experience" (*Psychoenergetic Systems*, 1975, Vol. 1, pp. 63-74), "but within the environment in which the organism is exposed." Thus, theorizing physical methods of generating telepathy and other psi phenomena is the wrong approach, Persinger claims. He rejects as unrealistic the idea that "the energy source of paranormal events originates within the organism and that something *leaves* one organism (the putative agent) and influences a second organism (the putative percipient)."

"It is highly unlikely that sufficient amounts of stimulus energy could originate and be generated from the body/brain to any significant effectual distance. Physically speaking, the amounts of energy within the brain/body are much too minute . . . . Paranormal phenomena utilize the energy already available in the physical environment."

The geomagnetic field, interacting with known solar radiations and perhaps the *superspectrum* of the Sun/black body binary system may be more subtle and complex than we realize or are capable of dealing with. It may be no mere coincidence, then, that the human brain wave cycle (eight per second) is in almost perfect synchronization with the propagation of radio, light, and all known electromagnetic radiation on this planet. EM radiation, for example, flashes completely around the globe exactly *eight* times in one second.

The UFOs, fireballs, spherical and cigar-shaped lights (and "objects"), and baffling atmospheric luminosities seen before, during, and after earthquakes and volcanic eruptions have also been detected from great distances during severe electrical storms. Scientists have theorized that violent low-level air oscillation, "caused in some unknown manner by earthquakes and storms, causes electrical luminosity in the atmosphere."

Former NASA scientist William R. Corliss points out in his book *Strange Phenomena* that these lights also appear when there is no earthquake, volcanic eruption, or electrical storm within thousands of miles.

How is such power generated, and how is it related to UFO and other phenomena? Trying to find a rational path through this maze is one of the most precarious positions for the physical scientist because extremely low-frequency EM radiation also affects his or her own thought processes and, at some as-yet-undetermined point, subtly blends with "nonphysical" or paranormal experience. It's virtually impossible to get an accurate measurement of something when your presence either interferes with the thing you are trying to measure, *or* when the object or location to be measured interferes in any way with the transducer that does the measuring—*the brain*.

In his article, "The Problems of Human Verbal Behaviour; The Final Reference for Measuring Ostensible Phenomena" (*The Journal of Research in PSI Phenomena*, Vol. 1, No. 1, 1976), Dr. Persinger observed that "human thought responses and related behaviours are the final measurement devices, the terminal reference points."

A clearer understanding of how electrical Earth currents modify the positive and negative ionization of the atmosphere (which influences the way we think, feel, and act) is necessary before we assert our much-cherished faith in complete freedom of will. Our democratic institutions promulgate the belief that man controls his own destiny (through man-made political, scientific, technological, religious, and other institutions), yet the evidence indicates that we are produced, sustained, nourished, and influenced by the Earth-Sun-Moon system. In turn, the Sun is powerfully affected by its retinue of planets.

Except for rare instances (i.e., Chinese seismologists in 1975), no one has reliably predicted the onset of an earthquake. And in spite of their success the previous year, the Chinese—for some unknown reason—were caught off-guard on July 28, 1976, when 750,000 Chinese died in history's third greatest earthquake catastrophe.

Experts in seismology are convinced that the most promising theory in earthquake prediction is intimately associated with the so-called piezo-electric effect, in which an electric potential is generated in certain kinds of quartz-bearing rock when it is subjected to stress, such as pressure. (The same principle is used in telephone receivers and microphone transmitters, in which varying pressures from sound waves cause corresponding electrical responses in the crystals.)

After a series of studies, two New York physicists, J. R. Powell and David Finkelstein, concluded that stress is accumulated in rocks in a fault zone over a period of years; this stress could change in intensity several days before a large earthquake—as well as during and after the quake.

These stress-intensity alterations seem to be detectable by animals. Scientists who once rejected such folklore as nonsense are now giving serious attention to reports of strange animal activity prior to earthquakes. Rats, for example, are said to have swarmed through the gutters of San Fernando the night before the great 1971 quake in California, and there have been other reports of similar mass evacuation of rats. In Florida, alligators scrambled out of the water and ran into the woods, "screaming all the while." The bizarre behavior of barnyard and domestic animals (reported in virtually every nation on Earth) indicates that our fellow creatures have some kind of physical or brain receptor site which enables them to know in advance that an earthquake is about to strike: geese fly into trees, pigs bite each other, and snakes, pigs, cows, and horses make frenzied attempts to flee *from* cover when an earthquake is imminent. This linkage of erratic animal behavior with advance earthquake warnings has been accepted among the peoples of most civilized nations—especially in the Far East—as thoroughly reliable for at least several thousand years.

Thus, when an American scientific delegation visited China in June, 1976, they were able to bring back proof that the Chinese actually did predict a major quake on February 4, 1975, at Haicheng in northeast China, thereby saving tens of thousands of lives. After a closed-door session in Paris, some American earthquake experts reported that the U.S. Geological Survey had issued a grant for "a long-range study of pocket mice and kangaroo rats to learn whether animals can sense upcoming earthquakes."

Dr. Durward D. Skiles, a geophysicist, and Dr. Robert G. Lindberg, a biologist, both from UCLA, then set up an informal desert laboratory at the southern edge of the "Palmdale Bulge," an area of frequent small tremors that is closely and constantly studied by seismologists. "The ideal payoff, scientifically speaking," said Skiles, "would be if all the mice came above ground at high noon and refused to go back into their burrows and all the rats raced on their running wheels at the same time, followed the next day by a major earthquake."

They are now convinced that any valid predictive system must rely on a *combination* of clues, including earth tilts, foreshocks, the release of gases from well water, changes in gravity, magnetism, electrical earth currents, ground water levels, *and* unusual *animal behavior*. (When they found the skeletons of three gophers buried in burrows in sediment a few feet below the surface that was offset by a quake that struck California approximately 6,000 years ago, scientists from the Geological Survey of the Department of the Interior concluded late in July, 1977, that the Ventura Fault is still potentially active.)

The strange lights seen in the skies over the Malagasy Republic on the island of Madagascar 500 kilometers off the coast of Mozambique on the night of July 30, 1977, left scientists in a state of stunned confusion. A "meteor" of vast size struck the Earth, producing "what must be the greatest impact crater of modern times." According to Agence France Presse, "a terrible noise" and "a bluish light" accompanied "meteoric fireballs" seen over Madagascar's capital city, Tananarive. Reports of a 240-meter crater were received in the Soviet Union and the United States. "This would be one of the major, if not *the* major, meteorite events of this century," said Harold Provenmire, assistant director of the American Meteor Society. A great flaming or bright object did flash through the skies over Madagascar, but no giant crater was found, although something enormous is known to have fallen in the area. A half hour later, an earthquake struck near Fianarantsoa.

By an odd twist of events, the Tananarive Seismological Observatory was "suffering from a defective machine"—a malfunctioning seismograph—at the time of the impact.

Whether they are "meteoric fireballs" or UFOs, spheroid or "flying saucer" luminosities are observed in the skies day and night and, *most important*, in areas where *no* seismic activity has been reported for months or years before (or after) the sightings. Such mysteries may indicate the working of an unspecified geophysical process which produces intense oval, spherical, and "platelike" displays of light.

Flying saucers, alien spaceships, and strange creatures reported by "contactees" (Betty and Barney Hill are, of course, the most famous) are regarded as apocryphal by most scientists. But the disturbing, unexplained similarities among the firsthand accounts of these events, especially those during the 1950s and 1960s coming from people with no knowledge of or interest in the details of others who shared the same experience, are puzzling.

So many motorists have reported being chased by luminous saucer-shaped "objects" displaying flickering red, blue, white, and green lights that the tendency of scientists to dismiss these recurring stories is very widespread. Yet why do the witnesses to UFOs so frequently report the stalling of their automobiles, the dimming of their headlights, the shorting-out of their cars' ignition systems? And why the familiar "sudden disappearance" and the "instant reappearance" in the sky sometimes three to five miles away, and the "impossible" right-angle turns of UFOs traveling at speeds of more than 2,000 miles an hour?

Other witnesses report the "surveillance activity" of UFOs following their cars, and many have been terrified by what seemed to them to be a sudden "attack" by the flying saucer, on vehicles carrying anywhere from two to six passengers.

Reports are one thing, but the evidence includes people known to have suffered from amnesia after the bizarre events—an amnesia that often lasts until they are hypnotized and "relive" their harrowing experiences. How do we explain the many UFO witnesses who emerged from the ordeal in a state of shock, temporarily blinded, or with long-lasting physical impairments such as edema ("skin burns"), nausea, inability to sleep, nightmares, eye swelling, and severe disturbances of the endocrine system—especially impotence and thyroid and testicular malfunction? Dr. Michael A. Persinger believes the same effects are possible from exposure to extremely low frequency (electromagnetic) fields in the area.

When a magic buff sees a new illusion, chances are that—unless he's a seasoned veteran with a comprehensive working knowledge of how such effects are generally achieved—he's just as baffled as the wide-eyed kids in the audience. He, however, differs from the amateur in one important respect: rather than working backward, trying to figure out how the trick was done, he asks: *If I wanted to achieve that particular illusion, how would I go about it?* From this point, he begins to develop his version of the illusion.

We can use the same approach with certain scientific mysteries. In this case, the phenomenon of Unidentified Flying Objects, which may be neither "objects," nor "flying," but simply *unidentified*.

Some researchers have discovered a recurrent connection between certain geographic and atmospheric locations and UFO reports. Instead of blindly struggling to unravel the puzzle of how "alien spaceships" are able to maneuver in our atmosphere at such blinding speeds, or how their glowing vessels can make physically impossible right-angle changes in course without being ripped apart, killing every living creature inside—or without even slowing down, we can apply the rule of Occam's Razor (i.e., the simplest explanation is probably closest to the truth) and try a theoretical model of Unidentified Flying Objects.

Using only the known, generally accepted principles of geophysics, electromagnetism, and a basic knowledge of human behavior, Dr. Michael Persinger has synthesized the effects of thousands of UFO-related adventures on the human brain (a living electromagnetic system) and inert matter.

Ever since their startling modern reappearance in 1947, UFOs have seemed to function through mechanisms so exotic and advanced that, by comparison, our fledgling space-age technology looked crude and cumbersome. Reports of these strange lights in the sky have been made in virtually every language, geographic location, and historical epoch. While some ancient people regarded UFOs as mystical harbingers of religious events (pillars of light by night, columns of clouds by day), other civilizations interpreted the luminous spheroids flashing through the atmosphere in terms of the prevailing beliefs of their culture.

In the Far East, for example, they were frequently looked upon as "dragons." Among Meso-Americans, UFOs were interpreted as symbols of various cultural gods and demons, and in the Mideast as "signs from God." Moreover, despite our own relatively advanced science and highly developed technology, we are not very different from our remote ancestors. In fact, we're still trying to decide whether the increased size of the human brain during a relatively short period (compared, say, to the much longer evolutionary stages of other mammals) is a result of adaptation to a radically changing environment or is due to the "commands" of the genetic structure tucked inside our brains and bodies.

According to a burgeoning discipline called sociobiology, Homo sapiens and all other forms of life are simply the result of different attempts by DNA and other molecular combinations to survive. Genes, the sociobiologists claim, don't give a hoot whether they make it into the future as owls, cockroaches, baboons, or humans; their sole purpose is *survival*. And their protective vehicles, according to this almost science-fictional view, are the gross, lumbering bodies of humans and other creatures which serve as robots to carry their genetic information.

In this context, the sobriquet "Unidentified Flying Objects" is simply the most convenient, easily understood concept of a civilization possessing an awareness that, with bigger rocket boosters, it can reach the planets—*precisely what man is doing*. "Extraterrestrial aliens" from greatly advanced federations of worlds, therefore, *must* be able to use their own exotic vessels to reach the Earth. Consequently, unidentified lights in the sky are uncritically accepted as spaceships from other stars and/or galaxies.

This concept is reinforced by mass media communication and firmly embedded in our collective consciousness. Almost any experience associated with a luminous atmospheric glow is, in the mind of the observer, instantly interchangeable with "UFO," which is consanguine to "intelligent extraterrestrial aliens."

The implicit popular assumption is that experiences identified by the same name must also have identical origins and operate according to the same mechanisms. Since no one has ever captured a "flying saucer," taken detailed photographs of its interior (or *exterior*), or returned with artifacts from a nonhuman technology following one of the reports of physical "contact with extraterrestrial aliens," the logical conclusion seems to be that the civilization(s) from which these "spaceships" originate must be infinitely superior to our own.

Such a concept is as real (and inevitable) to our civilization—which is itself on the brink of large-scale exploration of other planets—as "dragons," "demons," and "gods" were to the nomadic, religious, and agricultural societies of our remote ancestors.

Proceeding from just such a basis, two Canadian scientists, Dr. Michael Persinger and Dr. G. F. Lafreniere, collected more than 7,000 reports of strange and unusual events, including cases of UFOs, ghosts, poltergeists, examples of "psychokinesis," and other "Fortean" phenomena (i.e., the falling ice, frogs, metal, fish, meat, rocks, etc., from the sky) over a period of

160 years. When the data were classified, sorted by computer, and then analyzed, some rather conspicuous and significant patterns emerged.

The scientists quickly realized that clusters of reports about these anomalous events occurred in the same places at twenty-year intervals. More important, there was a strong tendency for worldwide patterns of similar strange reports to appear during the peak periods.

"It is often forgotten or unrealized," said Dr. Persinger, "that the human species exists upon an extremely thin semistable surface beneath which mammoth reactions and forces are constantly in progress. Some of these forces are represented upon the Earth's surface, e.g., the geomagnetic field. Still other forces are maintained within the crustal-mantle matrix and become apparent only during abrupt tectonic modifications, e.g., seismic activities." Although earthquakes are basically the mechanical slippage of surface "plates," Persinger found a significant number of reports associated with electromagnetism to provide the clues needed to start solving some of the mysteries about many UFO reports.

Strange lights on the ground or in the sky before, during, and after earthquakes (including "thunderless earthquake lightning") during the past few centuries were numerous enough to convince the scientists that earthquake-associated lights involved "(1) indefinite instantaneous illuminations, (2) bright flames and emanations, (3) phosphorescent-like sky or clouds, and (4) well-defined mobile luminous 'masses.'"

These "masses" or UFO-like apparitions thoroughly intrigued Persinger and Lafreniere. The metaphors used reflected the languages and cultures that described them: "pillars of fire," "flying luminous shields," and "funnel-shaped or trumpet-like glows" are often intimately associated with earthquakes. Other descriptions: "luminous wheels," "columns of whirling fire on mountains," "chains of spheroid glows moving in the same direction," and "fleets of glowing airships."

The physical details and other accounts of UFOs varied broadly. Multicolored balls of fire or light, for instance, appeared anywhere from more than twelve hours before to several minutes after earthquakes. Many of these glowing objects seemed, to the people who saw them, perfectly solid and able to maintain absolute stability in the sky or on the ground for long periods of time. When approached, many observers reported that the UFOs "suddenly moved upward and vanished," but not always directly or smoothly. The glowing spheroids often made right-angle turns and exhibited spectacular changes in color.

From these data the scientists conceived a model in which underground strains and the massive buildup of rock pressures (even when no earthquake followed) generated piezo-electric effects of more than 100,000 volts per meter—certainly more than enough to charge the atmosphere for great distances, vertically as well as horizontally.

These electrical fields (often distorted due to peculiarities of the natural "architecture" of the subsurface rocks) focused and intensified geophysical forces in certain places, with the result that otherwise mild electrical manifestations became abnormal. So much so, in fact, that some of the eyewitness accounts of UFOs not only made it seem as though the objects were somehow "alive," but that they also seemed to the observers to possess autonomy, consciousness, and—in some cases—"intelligence."

In the popular literature about flying saucers, the scientists weren't too surprised to see UFOs described not only as spaceships but also as "intelligent Beings" in their own right. These sightings were usually made in areas known to be subjected to tectonic stress and rock strain release, and usually had long histories of earth tremors. When the underground pressures reached critical stresses, intense electric fields were generated, resulting in "the formation of highly localized, transient column-like electric field formations." Inside these columns, the "transient ionization of the air" usually assumed the characteristic spheroid or ellipsoid/cylindrical shape because of local geophysical (and sometimes man-made) structures such as power lines, pipelines, and power stations.

The three-dimensional movement of the UFO luminosity, according to their explanation, made it seem as substantial as a hologram projection of a solid object, and it would reflect the vectoral changes in three-dimensional subsurface pressures and strain release. "The position of the luminosity," according to Dr. Persinger, "could display marked mobility, from almost perfect horizontal or lateral movement to sudden alterations in altitude in either vertical directions (into the sky or into the ground)."

The areas of the continental United States most prone to seismic activity, they found, were also the sites of the greatest number of reports of UFO sightings. In older pre-Columbian cultures, the UFOs were often referred to as "moving moons."

When these electromagnetic manifestations move through space they naturally cause an increase in EM disturbances. "Changes in or failures of radio transmission/reception, electrical appliances, lighting systems or compasses would be reported near the phenomena," according to Lafreniere and Persinger.

The direct physical effects on eyewitnesses, the good doctors claim, "could be more severe." Physical encounters with the UFO (electrical field), even when the field is not strong enough to generate a visible glow, often result in weird feelings of apprehension, fear, the raising of the hair on the body and head—"piloerection, and other unusual subjective behaviors associated with electrostatic fields of high intensity. Movement of the field toward the observer or of the human observer toward the column could induce currents sufficient to produce paralysis or unconsciousness; such experiences have been reported in the laboratory situation with direct current induction (Persinger, 1975; Beal, 1974; Herin, 1968)."

These are compelling interpretations of what happens to the human body, brain, and behavior when they are exposed to these naturally occurring seismic/stress-related electrical fields. (It may also be precisely what occurs when human beings encounter nonhuman beings whose "bodies" are pure *energy* instead of gross physical matter.) Here is the interesting conclusion of their report:

"The stimulation of the electrically unstable portions of the brain, such as the hippocampal formation, could allow the person access to imagery of epileptic, aura-like form. Such imagery would be intense and indistinguishable from 'reality.' Pre-event amnesia associated with the electric shock-induced alteration in consciousness could allow confabulation characterized by the person's beliefs and fantasies. Direct exposure to intense ionizing radiation associated with the discharge periods should be followed hours to days later by . . . 'skin burns,' eye swelling, nausea, temporary blindness, sleep difficulties and sexual disturbances."

Interestingly, and perhaps significantly, essentially the same explanation applies to people who "think they see ghosts, apparitions, and other paranormal phenomena."

When the facts are known, we may be surprised to learn that UFOs, ghosts, poltergeists, time machines, and other "unscientific" phenomena are exactly what they have always seemed to be (*viz.*, Occam's Razor). If the glowing discs observed throughout every historical period are *not* electrical atmospheric charges generated by the grinding of rocks prior to earthquakes (there are *numerous* holes in that theory), it poses two critical questions:

1. Why do committees for the scientific investigation of claims of the paranormal *never* make any scientific investigations?

2. Why do these scientists exert such efforts (through the authority they've bestowed upon themselves) to suppress honest investigation of things that they have declared "off limits" to the rest of us?

The fruits of modern technology are taken pretty much for granted. The poorest people in rural and inner-city areas, for instance, enjoy some luxuries beyond the wildest dreams of the richest sultans, czars, and kings of history. Caesar's mind would have boggled at photography, telephones, and color television. A small computer or digital watch would have astounded Isaac Newton. Ghengis Khan and Attila the Hun would have drooled over automatic weapons and troop-carrying helicopters. The sight of a modern surgical theater would probably have stunned Hippocrates, and it's doubtful whether Alexander the Great would have understood American democracy, orbiting satellites, or spaceships landing on the Moon and planets.

So why should we expect our "scientific" vigilantes to consider the possibility that UFOs may indeed be spaceships—or machines sent backward in time by historians from our own future?

CHAPTER 3

Supergiants and the Holy Solar Corona

Our life-giving Sun, a variable flare star, shakes and wobbles like a huge bubble in a gentle breeze. At present, it seems to be going through a period of perhaps severe abnormality. We exist in a violent, unpredictable Universe, and our familiar Sun seems less and less to be an exception to the rule. The most recent and chilling scientific studies indicate that our local star may not be what we've always believed.

According to lunar photographs and samples brought back by the Apollo astronauts, the whole surface of the Moon is glazed, indicating that during a fairly recent period—possibly about 1500 B.C.—the Sun suddenly and briefly flared out with one hundred times as much heat and energy as it usually generates. Since then, new evidence has shown that at one time the entire Earth *melted* and its geologic clocks were restarted.

On August 7, 1972, a solar flare blasted forth more energy then the entire United States could consume in 100 million years. Early in 1974, Skylab astronauts photographed a stupendous "bubble" of plasma erupting on the other side of the Sun. In July, 1975, a report to the National Science Foundation revealed that our star actually "flickers," and by studying light reflected by the outer planets, scientists discovered radical variations in the amount of heat and light emitted by the Sun. Such findings have raised ominous doubts about our star's equilibrium.

In less than two decades, some of science's most rigid dogmas have worn and cracked. It used to be nothing short of heresy—even "lunacy"—to suggest that the planets could possibly have any influence on the Sun and/or the Earth. Then two geologists, a Canadian, Claude Hillaire-Marcel of the Université de Quebec at Montreal and Rhodes W. Fairbridge of Columbia, made some surprising correlations (*Nature*, August 4, 1977) between "a shrinking, growing, 11-year sunspot cycle every 45 years," and the activity of the Sun and planets in triggering great climatologic changes on Earth. One of the outstanding periodicities turned up was 1,134 years long *"the time between conjunctions of the major planets."*

Another dogma, still alive and kicking, is that in spite of all the evidence to the contrary, nothing in the Universe can possibly exceed the speed of light—186,200 miles per second. Physicists have been known to gnash their teeth and utter dreadful oaths at the mere suggestion that pulsars, quasars, or galaxies (even the Starship *Enterprise*) could exceed the speed of light. "Even if two galaxies are moving away from each other at *more* than half the speed of light," insisted Dr. Mark Chartrand, a Hayden Planetarium astronomer with his own radio show, "you can't split the difference and come up with anything faster than light speed. It's just impossible."

Try telling a second-grader that when two cars, each doing fifty-five miles per hour, pass each other, their relative speed is only ninety miles per hour, and the kid will (or should) laugh in your face. But astronomers and physicists have been drumming this sort of thing into the minds of future astronomers and physicists since Albert Einstein's day.

Not only will the contradictory astrophysical conundrums not kindly go away, they keep piling up. Two "superluminary objects"—one traveling at five times the speed of light and the other at *eight* times light speed were observed early in 1979 by German astronomers. Unhappy as it makes many astrophysicists, and as contrived and foolish as their attempts to explain away these superluminal velocities seem, about half the known "strong, compact, very distant radio sources" *are* flying apart, pulsating, or speeding away from each other much faster than the established speed of light! At the Owens Valley Radio Observatory, three quasars and a galaxy were observed in August, 1977, to be reacting in this impossible manner.

I've always suspected that when a star goes nova, near-light speeds are approached, and when a star goes supernova, the speed of light is achieved by the outermost layers of the destroyed sun. Our Milky Way Galaxy is long overdue for a supernova. Astronomers say these dreadful (to us) natural events happen about twice a century. I'm not too sure about this because I haven't been watching the Galaxy that long, but their estimates are widely variable. If, say, a relatively nearby star, several hundred light-years away, exploded and destroyed itself in supernova violence, the night side of the Earth would be almost as bright as the day side—at least for a few months.

On September 7, 1977, X-ray sensors aboard Britain's Ariel satellite detected an explosion of catastrophic dimensions in the constellation Ophiuchus, the Serpent-Bearer. At the same time, an Anglo-Australian observatory in Siding Spring, Australia, was watching the explosion in visible light. Soon afterward, America's High Energy Astronomy Observatory, launched on August 12, 1977, confirmed the event.

According to Dr. Daniel A. Schwartz of the Center for Astrophysics, a sun like our own exploding like a hydrogen bomb increased the intensity of X-rays a thousandfold within a week. This made it the strongest known source of these radiations—with the exception of the constellation Scorpius.

Instead of a supernova, the explosion appeared to be a "nova," the term used by astrologer Tycho Brahe to describe a brilliant "new" star that flared up in the year 1572. Since then, it has been recognized that there are two basic classes of stellar explosion. Actually, the Tycho Brahe discovery of 1572 was a rare supernova—the collapse and explosion of a massive star that has exhausted its nuclear fuel. Supernovae are one-time events, whereas novas tend to recur. The latter probably originate in binary systems in which a giant star and a white dwarf are orbiting each other; at least this was the prevailing opinion until Dr. Edward Harrison of the University of Massachusetts announced in the British journal *Nature* that the Sun is orbiting a neutron star, a black dwarf or a black hole. The entire solar system is increasingly accelerating toward this body at a rate of close to half a million miles an hour.

Sunlight strikes the Earth's atmosphere in eight minutes but takes more than five hours to reach the outermost planet, Pluto. And if our nearest stellar neighbor, Alpha Proximi (whose light now takes four years to reach us), ever went supernova, all life on Earth and every other planet in the solar system would be vaporized.

So it may be wise to take a closer look at faithful old Sol—a medium-sized, rather complacent, and usually reliable star, because he has recently been showing such unusual signs of instability that astronomers are becoming increasingly concerned and puzzled. Today we are more acutely aware of cosmic conditions than we were just a few decades ago. In those days, a man on the Moon was pure science fiction. At this writing twenty-one Americans have been to the Moon and back. A dozen have landed, explored, and brought back pieces of our satellite.

Today the chief tourist attraction in Washington, D.C., is no longer the Capitol Building, the Washington Monument, or even the White House; by a margin of more than three to one, the most popular place is the National Air and Space Museum. Thus, as a people, we are preparing both psychologically and physically to launch our long odyssey to the planets and stars.

At the opposite end of the supernova spectrum there are mysterious event-places called black holes. The Universe may be full of them—often relatively small, utterly dark places where once-great blazing stars have become unstable or exploded, then collapsed in upon themselves through their own gravitational force and crushed their own atoms to the point that normal nuclear reaction was either stopped or became something else. According to the current guesstimates of astronomers, a star on the way to becoming a black hole may first have expanded to red gianthood, with a diameter ranging anywhere from dozens to hundreds of times that of our own Sun, which is a little over 864,000 miles across its equatorial region, more than 104 Earth diameters.

The star stuff then falls inward, sometimes with a great rush that results in a very dense white dwarf, a star so hot, its light so intense, and its material (while still technically in a gaseous state) so compacted under its own gravity that a teaspoonful of the star stuff would weigh hundreds of thousands of pounds—or *tons*.

The next step in this Jekyll-Hyde transition from red gianthood to black holedom is the further shrinkage from white dwarfdom to the neutrino star state where the atoms are compacted even closer—so close that their nuclei are squeezed together, almost touching.

Beyond that, say the experts who are supposed to know all that can possibly be known about such things, gravity simply becomes so intense that a condition variously known as a "singularity" or the "critical event horizon" becomes a theoretical reality.

Black holes seem quite literally to be "out of this Universe." British astrophysicist John Gribbin speculated that most of his colleagues have dabbled with black holes, either using them to explain away any puzzles in pet theories or invoking them as the basis of new theories of the Universe.

"We don't know, of course, what happens to matter that falls into a black hole," he wrote in the November, 1976, issue of *Astronomy*. "Conversely, a key question in astrophysics and cosmology has always been, 'Where does all the material in the Universe come from?' It's hardly surprising that some people should have tried to answer both questions at once by saying 'What goes in must come out,' and invoking the opposite of black holes to balance the Universe.

"The opposite phenomenon has been dubbed *white holes*, for obvious reasons. An even more graphic description would be cosmic gushers..."

Not a bad concept. Mysterious quasars, the blasting radio galaxies, even stars themselves, might be material from that other "non-Universe's black holes" exploding inward under their own gravitational pull to form the galaxies, stars, planets, and all other material in "our" Universe.

Black holes draw into themselves all matter within their gravitational sphere of influence (and that area is stupendously vast). Because the escape velocity from it *exceeds* 186,200 miles per second, nothing, not even light, can escape from a black hole. For the same reason, we can't jump off the Earth or even fly the most advanced jet beyond the Earth's gravitational field. Until some form of antigrav' device becomes a reality (possibly a form of electric propulsion engine), we'll continue to rely on the great chemical-gulping rockets to put our ships into orbit. The escape velocity to break free of the Earth's gravity is seven miles per second, as almost any schoolchild now knows.

But as far as we know, stars that have collapsed into black holes draw all surrounding energy and matter into themselves, and woe betide even the greatest of supergiant stars which have a black hole as a companion. The hole will draw off the star's outer "atmosphere," then its outer gases, and keep gobbling until there's nothing left of the star.

Theoretically.

Considering the sheer enormity of the largest known stars, that's no small accomplishment. Some of the greatest of the red supergiants are so colossal that their diameters, if they occupied the same space as the Sun, would engulf Mercury, whose orbit is 72 million miles across, Venus, with an orbital diameter of 134 million miles—and even the Earth, which is a mean distance of 93 million miles from the Sun. The *diameter* of the Earth's orbit, therefore, is more than 186 million miles. A star this big would be 200 times the size of our Sun.

Antares, the red supergiant in the "eye" of the constellation of Scorpius, is so vast that it would engulf and overlap the orbit of Mars (141,500,000 miles from the Sun) because it is more than 300 times as big as the Sun.

A still bigger star, over a *billion* miles in diameter, is VV Cephei. Light from one limb of Cephei takes well over four hours to reach its other limb. (It takes a little over *four seconds* for light to cross the Sun.) This star would engulf the orbit of gigantic Jupiter itself.

One of the still *more* impressive supergiants is Σ Aurigae which, if it occupied the Sun's position, would extend almost halfway between the orbits of Saturn and Uranus—almost *three billion* miles in diameter! Huge? Compare *that* to our Sun.

Of course, the mysterious quasars appear to be the most supercolossal objects in the Universe, but right now too little is known about them to draw any sort of conclusion that wouldn't be obsolete within a short time.

One great supergiant, Betelgeuse (Alpha Orionis), has blown off a shell of its own matter to dimensions exceeding 1,200 times its own 500-million-mile diameter. Betelgeuse, therefore, has extended its outer limits to more than 400 times the size of our entire solar system. Try to imagine a star so huge that light flashing at 186,200 miles per second cannot reach from one side of its supertitanic body—nearly three *trillion* miles—in less than 400 hours. That's sixteen days—more than two weeks!

Incomprehensible as it may seem, there are other objects far out in the Universe that dwarf even supergiants like Betelgeuse. On such a scale, our Earth seems less than insignificant.

Our Milky Way Galaxy is roughly 100,000 lightyears across, but there are also entire clusters of several thousand galaxies (each roughly like our own, with 200 billion or more stars) that until recently were believed to form the largest known objects in the Universe. A typical cluster is about three million light-years wide, meaning it takes light three million years to cross it; several are twice that size.

In 1974, Dutch radio astronomers using a multiple-antenna system, discovered an object beyond the constellation Leo Minor, far beyond our Galaxy and all of its thousands of neighbors, that is 18.5 million light-years wide, the biggest thing known in the Universe—so far.

Yet we congratulate ourselves on our great triumphs—our manned lunar landings and Moon exploration, our space robots probing the skin of Mars, our spaceships whipped around Jupiter and flung beyond Saturn—all televising back wondrous pictures of the mysteries of the outer gas giants even as they sail far out of the solar system. In spite of all these mighty efforts, however, *none* of our spaceships has managed to travel more than a mere fraction of the diameter of great Betelgeuse's outer shell.

At the other end of the scale, there are suns much smaller than our own—half its size, one tenth as large, even one hundredth the size of Sol. Some stars are considerably smaller than Jupiter—or even the Earth!

Red giants, blue giants, supergiants, and main sequence stars, dwarf stars, neutrino stars, black holes, and perhaps white holes—all of them man's nomenclature. The Universe is full of data, and we're just becoming sketchily aware that the vast store of knowledge we *believe* we possess is as nothing compared to that which awaits us out there.

Being human chauvinists and, as oxygen-breathing creatures, oxygen chauvinists, we're also Life-as-We-Know-It chauvinists and as such probably wouldn't be able to recognize an intelligent extraterrestrial nonhuman being if we walked right into one.

We're also Earth chauvinists and single Sun chauvinists because we know so little of double-eclipsing binary stars, for example; we speak of Sol as "our" star without knowing anything at all about the possible existence of life on Jupiter, Uranus, Neptune, or even Mars. Instead of it being our Sun, the exact reverse is true. The Sun's seemingly eternal, apparently invariable output of life-creating and sustaining energies makes us and every living thing in the solar system actually part of itself.

What do we really know about this life-giving star? We hardly ever give it a thought. "It's just there," and that's about the extent of our awareness. Just for now, though, let's stop taking the Sun for granted and attempt the awesome adventure of "tuning in" on this vast fusion furnace. Unfortunately, we lack the right senses to detect most of the superdynamic activity in and on our Sun. Whenever we do think about it, we see the Sun in our mind's eye as a silent, flat, yellow-white disc. It's anything *but* that.

There's *sound*, for example. Hardly anyone ever thinks of the "roaring" Sun. But *roar* it does!

There's no adjective hyperbolic enough in any language to describe the everlasting thunder of our "silent" Sun. But let's give it a try and do the best we can. Let's imagine we're in a heavily heat-shielded spaceship that lets us get even closer to our star than the orbit of the cratered innermost planet, Mercury. Let's zoom in like a comet, but instead of sailing along a trajectory that takes us completely out of the solar system (as the comets do—or seem to), we'll comfortably orbit, say, about 500,000 miles above the Sun's intensely hot, impossibly bright "surface."

What's the loudest noise you've ever heard? A cannon? A bomb? An earthquake? A tornado? I once sat thousands of yards away from a Saturn V rocket (Apollo 12), and when those gases ignited and liftoff began, the ground and the air quivered; nothing we've ever devised to record sound can duplicate the awesome, planet-thumping roar of a thirty-six-story-high tower of incandescent, gravity-defying force let loose in the atmosphere. By comparison, the loudest noise thunder can make is only a terrifying, but short-lived atmospheric boom; the Saturn V's thunder is *constant*. And yet, compared to a really heavy, dirty hydrogen bomb, the roar of the Saturn V is a mere trifle.

Watching the launchings of those great Apollo lunar ships on a television screen gave no real impression of what that was like. It usually showed a three- or four-inch-high rocket, and even in the closeups when you could see the flakes of frost shedding away from the hull around the liquid oxygen tank as the airframe trembled to ignition shock, you had no real idea of the awesome sound.

You might see the fast, hither-and-yon searching of the fire tongue as the gimballed motor responded to commands from the guidance device to keep the ship vertical, but little or no roaring of the mighty rockets came through. You couldn't feel the ground tremble as the blast cut loose, you couldn't hear the thunder of the gas stream because there's no electronic system built that can record and reproduce that sound.

An even greater sound blast is that of a relatively small hundred-kiloton atomic bomb. Some physicists try to convince us that the actual displacement of air molecules in a sound wave is negligible, but they don't usually consider sound waves with peak pressure of a few pounds per square inch and a half-cycle time of more than a second.

That's one *hell* of a blast! In the April, 1961, issue of *Analog*, science-fiction writer Hal Clement deplored his own lack of imagination about what it would be like when he was a few thousand yards from a small, forty-kiloton nuclear blast. He just wasn't prepared for its sheer violence: "It set the desert rocking under my feet with a set of ripples remarkably like those on a pond disturbed by a stone. It's a little disconcerting to have a trench which has been dug in hard soil seesaw like a raft in the wake of a speedboat."

He realized that his senses missed a great deal, both from the nuclear explosion and from the televised lift-off of a big rocket. "I remember it vividly . . . I can guess that I'm missing a good deal from the rocket takeoff picture, but can I *know* what I'm missing? My imagination isn't competent for the job.

"I could see, hear, feel, and smell, but those four senses don't cover a very wide band of phenomena. The radiation of four to eight thousand Angstrom electromagnetic photons; the broadcasting of atmospheric pressure waves at about all frequencies and energies which the properties of the air itself will permit; the transmission of shock waves to and through the solid ground; the fouling of the air with partly decomposed hydrocarbons and or hydronitrogens—is that all that's going on? Not on your tintype. That's merely all I'm personally equipped to detect."

Let's try for a closer look at the source of everything we are, the origin of the energy for all life that ever existed in this solar system. Moreover, let's do it with eyes not blindered by the dry, all-too-often lifeless facts and figures found in so many astronomy textbooks.

First of all, *is* the Sun a stable star? Is it somehow "programmed" to act in specific ways at certain times, or is Sol merely experiencing "beats" and cycles we haven't lived long enough as a species to observe and record? What is the Sun *really* like?

Without a filtered telescope it's almost impossible to see sunspots. Even with a good darkened lens, the image you see is a disc of light, visibly less brilliant away from the center and trembling noticeably at the edges. If you look very closely, you might detect large, irregular patches somewhat brighter than the overall disc, and perhaps the darker patterns of sunspots. That's about it. We're betrayed by our sensory and instrumental limitations. We hear, feel, and smell *nothing*. We can't even *see* everything. It's like watching a silent movie.

But a great star is not a silent thing.

With a better telescope and more intensive viewing you might catch a glimpse of the bubbling "rice grains" that show up on very narrow aperture filtered by the light of the hydrogen Alpha spectrum line. There are glowing faculae, vast prominences swirling, floating, fountaining upward and raining downward—seemingly out of sheer nothingness. Even so, it is still a ghostly, silent Sun.

(But stars are composed of matter, and matter has pressure—often *enormous* variable pressure—with equally impressive temperatures. This is all the propagation of sound needs to make every star in the Universe a roaring furnace. They vibrate like the Earth during an earthquake.)

Let's continue our voyage toward the photosphere. We'll "park" in orbit only a few thousand miles above the "surface." The sunspots are obvious; their rather cool penumbrae drop down to a relatively "chilly" 4,700 degrees Kelvin—the umbrae. What once looked like "rice grains" are now huge granules, brilliant mountainous humps a few hundred miles across and about 200 or 300 degrees hotter than the surrounding photosphere. They're like fast-changing hurricanes (a billion times more powerful than any terrestrial storm) that lose their identity in less than twenty minutes—sometimes ten.

Faculae are on a wholly different scale; first of all, they're brighter and thousands of miles across—sometimes *tens* of thousands. Their greater prominence and longer lives indicate that they're the tops of convective masses. Watch closely and you'll see the spicules, "infant" prominences (utterly fascinating to watch), as they flash upward for thousands of miles during their short lives. Great clouds of metallic gases, calcium vapor and hydrogen, float motionlessly 25,000 miles or so above the photosphere. They form into shifting, wavering, dancing columns, pillars, and fountains in some places, and gossamer curtains in others. They blast upward in some places and drift or rain downward elsewhere. For some reason the downward motion is predominant.

Surprisingly, the solar medium is extremely thin, only a few thousandths as dense as the Earth's atmosphere at sea level. But it is, after all, *material*—and it is *hot*. Let's move our heatproof, soundproof ship even closer and turn on our audio sensors—*very* carefully.

The full brunt of what we're about to hear would be totally deafening. Even at the lowest possible level you now realize that this is no silent movie. It's so ear-splitting that the most avid acid-rock fan would wince in pain.

Incredible cracks, shrieks, hisses, rumbles, growls, booms, hums, thunder—sounds for which no words have ever been invented. Even the continuous roar of 10 million hydrogen bombs going off consecutively couldn't be detected in this bellowing hell.

Just when you decide it is physically intolerable and reach to switch the sound off completely, the ship is rocked and you are bowled over by an explosion, a bang, nothing less than the planet-splitting crack of a colossal volume of gas speeding up from deep beneath the photosphere until it achieves supersonic speed—both for itself and the surrounding gas. It's virtually like the explosion of 10,000 tons of dynamite going off inside a huge steel vault—except that it's billions of times worse. Without the protective damping unit, you would be in total shock and permanently deaf.

You've become accustomed to the quick brightening of a huge hydrogen-calcium flocculus—one of those clouds of gas hanging in almost deathlike stillness several thousand miles over the photosphere. Suddenly it becomes brighter than before and much, much hotter—and *still* brighter. A few minutes before it was a darker shadowy thing against the more brilliant "surface." Suddenly we're grateful for the ultra-optical instruments because we're not going to see the whole story by light alone. There is, of course, light—from soft X-rays to the longest possible radio waves, but now, even with the sound sensors turned completely off, the superinsulated hull of our powerful spaceship is unable to dampen what's coming.

This is *really* a bang—if such it can be called—a BIG bang, but unlike an explosion, it just won't quit. Every microsecond it becomes louder as atoms are smashed madly against each other. Electrons are broadcast at light speed and strike others, which rebound endlessly in a savage spit of radiation. Nuclei are stripped and hurtle at half the speed of light out of the ionized region. Driving upward at nearly 500 miles a second, the flocculus, a blazing bubble of gas, hot even by solar standards, expands enormously. It's sheer hard work done against the local force fields, and the radiation strives mightily to rob the huge mass of its energy.

The noise almost drives you mad. But there are also prominences to see. If the "falling" stuff in these prominences is moving downward, why isn't it accelerating at something like thirty Gs? Gravity should do that to it, but it isn't. Some of the stuff just hangs there without falling at all. Gravity can't be *that* weak just a few thousand miles above the photosphere! Sunspots are cooler and quieter than the rest of the "surface."

Foremost among the thousands of questions that flash through your mind is the mystery of why a quiet prominence, a flocculus, which has been drifting peacefully—like a dark shadow against the roiling "surface"—jumps spectacularly from 40,000 degrees Kelvin to 200,000 degrees, then 900,000—and suddenly—what? Two *million?*

The known, accepted temperature of the photosphere used to be 3,000 or so degrees. Now astrophysicists have doubled that figure and talk about the temperatures of solar prominences running up to 30,000 to 40,000 degrees and coronal temperatures ranging between 800,000 in the quiet regions to four million or more in the really disturbed places.

Anywhere from four to a thousand atoms to the cubic centimeter is probably a better vacuum than any laboratory has yet produced. If even a few of those atoms are ionized or charged, the charge can travel, and when it does, it produces an electric current and a magnetic field.

The number of electrons inside a star is much higher, but so is the star stuff; therefore, you still have ions and electric currents. Because of the high ion concentration in our star, electrical conductivity is far better. Inside the Sun that plasma is moving—and violently—so it's inescapable that magnetic fields whip around the solar sphere from pole to pole and that those fields are powerful enough to influence everything within the life zone of Sol—however far out that may be.

Every once in a while, the fields of the Sun actually reverse polarity. Not long ago the field in the southern hemisphere did just that, but the star's northern hemispheric field didn't. There were two rather weak north poles, and this strange state of affairs didn't get back to normal for almost an entire year.

But let's return to that flocculus, the quiet prominence that suddenly exploded with an energy equivalent of 15 trillion atomic bombs, which is roughly equal to the total energy output of the Sun's entire surface in, oh—two fifths of a second. But it was almost a second Sun because it took the flare over half an hour to unload all that energy. That much power is more heat than there is at any one time in the whole territory outside the photosphere, chromosphere, and corona *combined!* The amazing thing is that the 4,000,000 degree corona wasn't in the least bit drained of heat to feed the flare.

A swirling tornado of incandescent gases 30,000 miles in diameter speeding upward at about 700 miles a second in a couple of minutes might seem to be abnormal, but it isn't. Performances like this happen fairly regularly. (We'll get to the *really* scary stuff in a later chapter.)

In this great flare the highest energies among the particles are on the order of 10 billion to 100 billion electron volts, but the really *hot* end of the cosmic ray spectrum doesn't seem to come from the Sun at all. It may have something to do with gravitational and other interplanetary energy factors, but some scientists are convinced that it doesn't originate within the solar system at all.

This is a whole new ballgame—one of the most promising fields for future research. I just don't know enough about the math of magneto-hydrodynamics, but there's a pair of torus-shaped magnetic fields circling beneath the photosphere of the Sun like a pair of bicycle tires, one in each hemisphere, but not exactly parallel to the Equator; they're rather like the stitch pattern of a tennis ball or a baseball, according to British astrophysicist John Gribbin.

Convection currents not only cut across these fields but slow down the currents and move the fields up and down as the Sun rotates, which creates an interesting effect on the Earth and other planets. In 1972 and 1973, the Orbiting Solar Observatory (OSO) 7 and the Skylab-Apollo Telescope missions were able to make extensive observations of a new phenomenon: *holes* in the Sun's superhot corona (that's the bright halo seen only during total solar eclipses).

A three-year study by the Naval Research Laboratory, the Kitt Peak National Observatory, and the Los Alamos Scientific Laboratory "showed that the solar wind doubled its speed past Earth nearly every time a coronal hole moved across the Sun's disc." This provided scientists with conclusive evidence that coronal holes, high-speed solar wind streams, and magnetic storms on the Earth are related.

If you're puzzled by the discrepancy between the stated twenty-five-day spin of the Sun and the twenty-seven-day "solar rotational period," that's because it takes about two and a half days for material expelled from the Sun to reach the Earth. Now scientists can predict *geomagnetic* storms about a week in advance—the time it takes a coronal hole to move across the face of the solar disc from its eastern edge to the center—plus the extra two and a half days Sun-to-Earth travel time for the plasma to reach us.

Skylab astronauts watched the holes form and grow as the solar wind rose and fell with them. Dr. A. J. Hundhausen of the High Altitude Observatory of the National Center for Atmospheric Research called it "absolutely amazing." Observing the holes over a period of time reveals that they grow and decay in patterns of three: a new one will appear 120 degrees west of an old one, which suggests that the modal pattern of the Sun's magnetic field probably conforms to the "tennis ball" analogy of John Gribbin.

The pattern rotates with the Sun's equatorial rotation rate, which is different from the spin of the Sun's atmosphere. Our star, therefore, has magnetic modes that rotate with a different speed from that of its atmosphere. "That's weird," says Dr. Hundhausen, "but physically possible . . ." The whole surface has spun up. What *that* means and whether it will ever spin down again is a mystery for future scientists to ponder.

CHAPTER 4

Electromagnetic Pollution: The Wild Kingdom on a Rampage

In the spring of 1976, tens of thousands of scarlet tanagers crash-landed all over the state of Maine. On Prince Edward Island in Nova Scotia, 400 desperate Canadians defended themselves against five million attacking crows. In May, 1977, along 300 miles of California coastline (from San Luis Obisbo through San Francisco to Shasta County), millions of what were believed to be gray Vaux swifts flew by the hundreds into the chimneys of inhabited homes. According to Connie Spain of Visalia, the dive-bombing birds "had long, black, skinny tail feathers and beady little eyes. We have about ten to twelve feet of solid birds in our house," she reported.

On June 1, 1977, thousands of sharks converged off the Gulf Coast resort of Corpus Christi, Texas, and drove terrified bathers from the 85-degree waters. Wave after wave of man-eating hammerheads were spotted by Coast Guard helicopter crews. The school of sharks stretched for almost twenty-five miles. Then at high noon, as quickly as they had come, the sharks disappeared.

But the following morning they were back in even greater numbers. John Wakeman of the University of Texas Marine Science Institute said he had counted as many as 2,000 sharks "and that's only a broad estimate." Stewart Springer, a marine biologist with Sarasota's Mote Marine Laboratory in Florida said it was unlikely that the sharks spotted on June 2nd were the same as the huge school of the previous day.

"They're a second wave," said Springer, "and that surprises me because I've never heard of more than a few hundred sharks together at any one time in the entire Gulf of Mexico. Contrary to the popular belief that sharks are only scavengers, these monsters are predators."

At the same time, a docile elephant in the Bronx Zoo started grabbing children and adults and pulling them through the bars of its cage—intent on mayhem. In London, another elephant went wild. Neither animal could be pacified. Now killers, each was dispatched with poison. On June 7, 1977, keeper Darrell Johnson was killed by an elehpant in the Franklin Park Zoo in Boston. In the spring of 1977, a bull elephant attacked and tried to kill his handler, Patricia Barbeau, on a movie set in Palmdale, California. Five other elephant-gone-mad incidents became news items later that summer.

Some experts contend that changes in the ion count of the atmosphere affect both human and animal activity and that our bioclocks (regulated by external forces) influence the biochemical, physiological, and behavioral activities of all living things. Among hundreds of other functions, these clocks influence body temperature, blood count, hormone levels, resistance to drugs, reaction to anesthetics, and tolerance to alcohol.

Many of these cyclic activities are influenced by gravitation and by electric, magnetic, and other yet-undiscovered energies—all emanating from the Sun and influenced in turn by the complex interaction of the planets.

"We have overwhelming evidence that some kinds of environmental forces must exist that alternately stimulate and depress mankind in the mass," said Edward R. Dewey, the foremost authority on cycles. "These same forces also affect plant life, animal life, even the weather . . . there are hundreds of cycles which, for one reason or another, cannot reasonably have an internal cause. In such cases we are forced to conclude an external cause. Various cycle periods are due to the complexities and interactions of the bodies of the solar system and with other extraterrestrial forces."

This was basically the same conviction held by Nikola Tesla, the electronic wizard who, at the turn of the century, constructed a 200-foot tower in Shoreham, Long Island, and—amazingly—succeeded in charging the entire planet with electricity. The pundits of his day called it a violation of natural laws, and the great financial backers of Tesla's startling experiment (who could no more capitalize on the free production of electricity than they could sell the air we breathe) ordered the great tower destroyed.

"Interplanetary electricity" of multi-hydrogen-bomb force was hypothesized by Immanuel Velikovsky, in his book *Worlds in Collision*, as being partially responsible for the great disasters of ancient times. It now appears that electromagnetic saturation of the terrestrial environment may have unforeseen, possibly disastrous effects on all living things, and that this electromagnetism is man-made.

"There's a strong possibility that man's superior brain and technology could be triggering a profound reaction from Nature," said a spokesman for an international group of wildlife observers.

The evidence supporting this chilling theory is so overwhelming that the Smithsonian Institution in Washington, D.C., was galvanized into action. In 1968, it hastily formed a supranational network of worried scientists who have been pooling information on every radical biological and geological event ever since. Lately they've become more gravely concerned than ever.

In keeping a watchful and worried eye on the ecosphere, here's a small sample of what they've turned up: swarms of bluefish and jacks churned up the waters of crowded beaches in Florida, attacking people and biting chunks of flesh from screaming bathers . . . an invasion of Canadian lynxes and wolves spilled across the northern border into the United States . . . a mysterious infestation of ineradicable African snails is growing annually in Miami . . . billions of dangerous and unpredictable hybrid Brazilian bees, whose sting often causes death, are beginning to swarm into Panama and Central America en route to the United States . . . Australia and Asia are intermittently besieged by unprecedented plagues of mice . . . a growing red tide of toxic algae persistently blooms along the shores of industrialized nations, poisoning shellfish and attacking the central nervous systems of people who eat oysters, clams, and other crustaceans.

In the beginning, such reports were regarded as freaks of Nature or once-in-a-lifetime incidents. But as the data poured in, an ominous suspicion began to grow in the minds of naturalists. We may now have the first subtle clues that, through an enormous abuse of atomic or electromagnetic radiation, the entire ecology of Earth has become unhinged, with more and more lower life forms reacting adversely. In some cases, whole schools or herds of animals seem to be afflicted with some strange disease that alters their normal behavior.

More and more psychologists are speculating that the course of human civilization itself has been drastically altered. Bizarre as this sounds, there's enough scientific evidence to support such an idea. The new Smithsonian Institution organization, based in the nation's capital, is composed of scientists from every discipline. It is the first time in history that such a group has been created—and the first indication that we could be facing an unprecedented—and undreamed of—threat, a synchronized onslaught.

The list of strange events unearthed by the Smithsonian's international scientific sleuths has triggered the suspicion of several governments that within a few years mankind may be under siege. During the last ten years there has been an increase in attacks against human beings by creatures ranging in size from bees to large carnivores.

Reports include attacks on man and his property by bears, pumas, lions, wolves, coyotes, lynxes, rats, birds, skunks—even fish and domestic dogs and pigs. Surprisingly, the most violent behavior has come from animals that had never before been hostile to man.

This rebellion of nature has astonished biologists. They simply cannot fathom the erratic behavior patterns of African snails, Brazilian bees, locusts, gnats, flies, and whole armies of rampaging ants. The Smithsonian Institution's Center for Short-Lived Phenomena (CSLP) would like to know whether Nature is becoming erratic or if these anomalies are a direct and inevitable result of industry, technology, and electromagnetism.

According to one theory, Nature automatically strives to neutralize pollution. Rivers, streams, and lakes cleanse themselves, if left alone long enough. This suggests deeper systems in Nature whose delicate balances have not been discovered. Not long ago, in addition to the "normal" fouling of the air we breathe and the water we drink, the only other man-created pollution we knew about was radioactive fallout. Then came the discovery of noise pollution. The suspicion now is that *electromagnetic* (EM) pollution, which affects every living thing, is more dangerous than any other kind and could be responsible for the widespread changes in animal behavior.

According to the White House Office of Telecommunications Policy (OTP), this electromagnetic pollution, the "waste" from the energy that runs our complex civilization, could be the source of unhealthy radiation that affects the brains and behavior of every living thing—from humans to insects and microbes.

Electrical power lines, radio and television transmitters—even microwave ovens—all discharge electromagnetic radiation into the atmosphere, the water, and soil. The widespread use of power by modern civilization has saturated the environment with EM radiation. It is now continually present in the air around every urban area. The countryside, rivers, lakes, and coastal areas are not immune either.

Just how EM pollution could trigger a worldwide attack on coral reefs by the voracious Crown of Thorns starfish, however, remains a mystery. And it takes considerable stretching of the imagination to blame electromagnetism for herds of wild moose that suddenly invaded populated urban areas of Anchorage, Alaska, or the swarms of locusts that recently devastated 250,000 square miles of farmland and forest in the Sudan. In the southeastern United States, an estimated 20 million gray squirrels exploded through half a dozen states. In Peru, an eruption of a chewing ant called *Atta sexdens* wiped out the tea and cocoa crops in 1975 and 1976. Over 164 attacks by rabid foxes, raccoons, and skunks were recorded in 1976 by the Delmar Wildlife Research Laboratory in New York State alone.

Are these just unrelated coincidences, or—as the experts believe—are they the result of electromagnetic saturation of the environment?

Let's take a closer look. Every so often the ocean erupts somewhere; fire and smoke blaze from the water into the sky and startle observers on passing ships (every such incident is duly reported by the Center for Short-Lived Phenomena). These are caused by subterranean volcanic eruptions that often build up to form new islands. But in the Philippines when thousands of acres of dark, wet tropical soil turned into a gigantic smoldering firebed, the explanation was "spontaneous combustion caused by hydrocarbons in the soil."

The ground was so hot that it killed every living thing except the much-feared *chirimach* insect, which is responsible for a deadly illness called Chagas' disease. These horribly poisonous insects are immune to every known pesticide and are all but impossible to control, much less eradicate. The population explosion among these insects and the consequent outbreak of Chagas' disease has resulted in illness or death in thousands of Filipinos.

And the disease is spreading. The most discouraging fact is that Chagas' disease is one of the few known plagues for which there is no vaccine.

"If I didn't know better," said a British entomologist, "I'd swear that something was manipulating certain kinds of bugs and turning them against humans. I don't know what to make of it. There's been a frightening change in the sex habits of bedbugs, for example. It's happening everywhere at once."

That was, at best, an understatement. The proliferations of bloodsucking bedbugs on a global scale is the result of what entomologists term "fantastic and prolonged sexual orgies" among these insects.

It sounds rather funny, but not to Canadian and American scientists who recently observed an evolutionary "first" among insects: the male bedbug has grown a sawlike device on its genitalia. In his constant sexual frenzy, the male ignores the female orifice. Instead, he slashes and saws his way into her abdomen and deposits his sperm for quick fertilization of her eggs. For some unfathomable reason, the entire species has suddenly developed incredible sexual stamina. They spend almost all their time mating with every bedbug in sight or scent—male *or* female.

Most amazing of all, though, is the fact that even the slashed and "raped" males are now laying fantastic numbers of eggs.

Nothing even close to it has ever been seen in the history of science. Some entomologists have ominously warned that such a radical change in the insect world may foreshadow a gigantic natural revolution that will ultimately affect man's future.

In several Florida cities a gigantic African snail called *Achatina fulica* has grown into an invasion force covering hundreds of acres of residential land. In spite of full-scale combat by state and federal pest eradication and control bureaus, the local snail populations are out of control.

What do the clouds of flies that blacken the English countryside, the swarms of poisonous bees, and the pods of whales that have recently been committing suicide all over the world—all part of the same ecological system—have in common? As many as thirty-five to sixty whales at a time regularly kill themselves by swimming full-speed ashore and beaching themselves. One of the favorite sites for this weird "ceremony" is close to former President Richard Nixon's San Clemente estate; during a recent mass suicide, thirty-seven of the huge mammals were strewn along the high-tide mark for almost half a mile. Immediately thereafter, scores of whales beached themselves on the Atlantic coast.

According to the Naval Undersea Research and Development Center, "the skin from their flukes and heads was chewed off, presumably due to thrashing, postmortem degeneration and tidal action." The initial implication was that bloodthirsty sharks in a feeding frenzy had ripped the entrails from the helpless whales, but this is now regarded by those who should know as a fiction. Sharks are known to avoid the huge creatures unless they are very young and solitary or sick, wounded, or helpless adults that have strayed from the group. Admittedly, the Earth is full of new mysteries. Off the coasts of Australia, Africa, and Asia, certain kinds of shark seem to be *seeking out* human flesh, judging from increased reports of shark attacks against humans. Yet on the Australian coastline near Gunnamatta, where no sharks have been reported or sighted, pods of whales continuously beach themselves and die. "They accidentally trapped themselves" is the explanation most often heard. However, the coastline is straight ocean beach for several miles with low rocky headlands at either end of Gunnamatta. It shelves away to a depth of ten fathoms within a half mile of the shore. Accidental entrapment is, therefore, out of the question as an explanation. The whales seem to be *deliberately* committing suicide; but if so, *why*?

In mid-1976, the densest population of jumbo squid ever seen spread out for a distance of at least 100 miles off the coast of California. All the sandy beaches along the coastline were covered with squid two to three feet in length. An even larger squid, *Dosidicus gigas*, which reaches an adult length of twelve to thirteen feet, invaded the entire coastlines of Panama, Chile, Peru, and across the tropical Pacific Ocean. The invasion reached a peak at the end of July when fishermen, who were taking them by the millions, reported the virtual disappearance of perch and anchovy from the waters.

From Delaware to Florida on the Atlantic Coast and Mississippi on the Gulf of Mexico, the ocean was turned into a sea of aspic during an outbreak of "cabbage head" jellyfish. The jellyfish explosion lasted from May to September of 1976. Trawlers' nets, left in the water for only fifteen minutes, raised tons of the creatures. North and South Carolina, Georgia, Florida, and the Gulf Coast waters "seemed like solid, colorless Jell-O pudding," according to the captain of a flotilla of boats from the Carolinas. Fortunately, *Stomolophus meleagris* or "jelly ball" is nonvenomous.

Canada has an invasion of lynxes; there are very worrisome plagues of mice in Australia and an explosion in the Spanish (olive) fly population. There is a ballooning red tide in New England and the lower Atlantic coast. The northward migration of deadly, hybridized Brazilian bees is inexorable; this exceedingly dangerous bee, formerly native to Africa, can prove fatal to animals and humans. In fact, their uncountable numbers, naked aggressiveness, which results in unprovoked mass attacks of venomous stinging and unpredictable swarming, strikes fear into the hearts of the bravest people. These bees have already crossed the Amazon and are heading for the Panama Canal Zone and Central America. Apiarists estimate that within a few years the Brazilian bee will be swarming throughout the southeastern United States.

Are these creatures *attracted* to the stronger electrical and magnetic fields of the more industrialized areas? Whatever the answer may be, some scientists are now afraid that prolonged exposure to electromagnetic radiation can have a negative effect on the health, behavior, and even genetic structure of animals *and* humans.

For example, Dr. W. Ross Adey of UCLA's Brain Research Institute has discovered that radiation at frequencies very similar to those of brainwaves (often produced by power lines and heavy electrical equipment) causes animals to become disoriented and often hostile.

In 1974, after a five-year pilot study on the effects of electromagnetic pollution conducted by the White House Office of Telecommunications Policy and thirty-three universities, Congress was warned that "We have entered an era of energy pollution . . . comparable to the chemical pollution of the environment."

Some of the scientists' worst fears have already been confirmed. The evidence gathered during controlled studies on the behavior of animals has forced government energy experts to reevaluate all previous safety standards for human and animal exposure to EM radiation.

Electromagnetic pollution runs the gamut of the entire radio spectrum: microwaves, medical diathermy units, radar, medium to ultra-high frequency radiation from radio and television transmitters, and low to extra-high frequencies from military communications systems and commercial aviation and shipping.

If the intensities of all these forms of radiation are high enough (as in a microwave oven), they can kill by generating heat deep within living tissues; it influences the cells of the brain and central nervous system and affects the behavior pattern of every organism. It seems reasonable, therefore, that it may, in some way, interfere with the known and unknown forces and energies generated by the Sun.

Long-term exposure to electromagnetic radiation has produced extremely adverse effects on rats. Psychologist Susan Korbel of Harper College in Illinois, who made the observations, claims that similar studies in the Soviet Union indicate that EM pollution breaks down enzymes, the extremely vital chemicals that control many biological functions—*especially the activity of the brain.*

Conversely, other studies have shown the *beneficial* side effects of *low-current* electrical charges in the healing of injuries and illnesses. Humans, as well as all other living things, *need* the normal, natural geomagnetic field for our well-being and health. We also need the natural electromagnetism of the atmosphere we breathe and the steady flow of solar energy.

At any given time, roughly 2,000 thunderstorms are raging somewhere on the planet. These electrical storms contribute to the ionization of the air which promotes our general health. This is vastly different from EM saturation of the environment. The long-range effect of this kind of saturation on terrestrial life forms seems to be very bad—in some cases perhaps deadly.

EM pollution has spread throughout our atmosphere—in the soil and the waters of our lakes, rivers, and oceans. At any given time, about three tons of airborne insects exist in each cubic mile of atmosphere in the temperature zones. Our planet's soil also harbors thousands of species of animals and insects, many unclassified and often undiscovered but essential nonetheless to the chain of life. By a wide margin, the oceans harbor most of the life forms on Earth, although little is known about teeming animal and plant colonies in rivers, lakes, bays, and the deepest parts of the oceans.

"Something strange is affecting much of the Earth's great creature population," said British researcher Egerton Sykes. He seemed bewildered by the unprecedented series of unprovoked and often savage attacks on man by animals previously considered harmless. "This is only speculation," he said, "but it could be caused by changes in the electrical current of the planet."

In May, 1974, a 200-pound, very peaceful St. Bernard named Caesar attacked and killed a six-year-old boy in East Islip, Long Island. A series of similar attacks by formerly docile pets was climaxed a week later on May 30, 1974, when eleven-year-old Brian Coleman of Mastic, Long Island, stood waiting for his school bus. Out of nowhere, a 180-pound St. Bernard, which was owned by a gas station operator, viciously attacked and tore at the child's flesh.

According to newspaper accounts, in Illinois, Ohio,

and New York in August, 1975, a series of attacks by St. Bernard and German shepherd dogs against children baffled police, dog owners, and ASPCA officials.

In mid-October, 1975, two elderly people were savagely attacked in New York by their own German shepherd dogs. "I can't understand it," an investigating officer said. "I knew both these people and they had the gentlest dogs imaginable." (Several almost identical dog attacks occurred elsewhere in New York City at the same time.)

The citizens of Prince Edward Island in Nova Scotia, under attack by five million shrieking crows, waged a week-long battle against the marauders with shotguns, cannon, rifles, dynamite, brooms, rakes—anything at hand. Many were wounded, suffered from severe exhaustion, nervous breakdowns and heart attacks.

In 1974 a sudden resurgence of the Norway rat horrified residents of the town of Carpentersville, Illinois, which has a population of 25,000. The number of Norway rats quickly outnumbered the humans ten to one. With 250,000 of the large rodents running wild, mere existence became a living nightmare.

Then, the latest in a weird series of "blood-curdling frog wars" erupted in Malaysia between two "armies of frogs." In mid-June, 1974, when a widespread infestation of leaf-cutting and driver ants spread through the Sudan, swarms of locusts crossed the sky, blotted out the flaring Sun, and spread over the countryside, devouring crops, destroying millions of acres of flora, and deepening the already profound hardship inflicted by the African drought. Next, in 1975, according to a report by the Soviet Academy of Sciences, there was a repetition in Russia of the Victorian mouse plague that had previously occurred in Australia.

"For some unknown reason," said a Soviet scientist, "we are seeing significant and direful changes in most biological and ecological systems. We are witnessing rare and unusual animal behavior, strange migrations, sudden explosions of insect and animal populations, and increasing mortality rates among humans."

Whenever the Earth quakes somewhere, the entire planet "rings like a bell" and oscillates with an enormous number of frequencies. From studying these vibratory effects, seismologists have built a detailed picture of the planet's interior structure.

Seismic studies of the pulsating, flaring, oscillating sun have revealed that it quakes and wobbles like a floating bubble, averaging minor oscillations at five-minute intervals, but with thousands of other small starquakes lasting as long as an hour. There was one report of a regular wobble with a two-hour-and-forty-minute period.

These seismic soundings of the Sun are proving to be valuable tools to probe the deep interior of our star as well as the more complex surface features. The result: an admission that the Sun's five-minute behavior is a *global* wobble and not just some local surface reaction. Physicists at the University of Arizona have also found temperature perturbations coinciding with the Sun's many oscillatory modes that have been nothing short of shocking. Not shocking enough, however, for the scientists to correlate the angular positions of the planets with this newly discovered solar activity—or, for that matter, to avail themselves of Dr. C. G. Abbot's *Periodicities in Solar Physics and Terrestrial Meteorology* (which, incidentally, was published in Czechoslovakia and the Soviet Union in 1938 when Dr. Abbot was Secretary of the Smithsonian Institution).

Countless billions of life forms existing in this astoundingly complex terrestrial eco-sphere are indeed affected by variations in solar energy output, including electromagnetic and myriad other forces. Trillions of species of airborne creatures, underground microbes, nematodes, and thousands upon thousands of insect families, surface dwellers ranging in size from the microscopic to huge mammals, and the numberless interacting creatures of the seas, oceans, and all other waterways must also be affected by the increasing levels of man-made electromagnetic pollution.

Exactly *how* this infinitely complex interaction of

STORM ON THE SUN

Simple, the man said.

The nearest star is the Sun. All terrestrial and whatever life there may be on the other planets of this system owes its existence to the electromagnetic and other radiations from our star. In effect, all our functions, all that we *are*, in fact, is due to—and part of—the solar *superspectrum*.

Until quite recently, all that scientists knew about our local star came from studies of its surface. Then physicists began formulating mathematical models of the Sun's interior, but they ran into a monumental problem. According to the structure, they theorized, energy is supposed to be produced in the very center of the star (the so-called neutrino core) and radiated outward into the convective zone (still inside the Sun).

As the star converted hydrogen into helium, the outward push of the heat/energy generated at the core of this huge nuclear fusion furnace is balanced by the immense gravitational force, which helps maintain the Sun's equilibrium and at the same time creates the pressures that have kept the Sun "burning" so evenly for billions of years. (This is just a brief, simplistic explanation of what we think we know about the Sun's physical life.)

Energy is carried up into the chromosphere and then to the photosphere—the visible surface. According to the mathematical theory it takes from one million to ten million years for photons (light particles) to fight their way through the Sun's 432,000-mile radius to the surface. This is the most widely accepted belief among scientists. It implies that sunspots and solar flares are the result of "pieces of magnetic field which, after being buried inside the Sun for hundreds of years, have risen to the surface."

But like most dogmas, this one is wrong. Few solar physicists who know about it will concede that John H. Nelson the astronomer and radio weather forecaster for RCA, Incorporated (the world's largest long-distance communications network) was the first to predict exactly when sunspots, solar flares, and other magnetic storms will appear. These cause great storms in the highest reaches of the Earth's atmosphere—the ionosphere—and garble or destroy short-wave radio broadcasts.

Nelson made these forecasts for RCA with an amazing record of accuracy for about thirty years before he retired to continue working as a consultant. Solar flares and sunspots could *not* have existed inside the Sun for centuries *before* Nelson was born because he predicts their appearance months, even days before they appear. His forecasts are based on the angular positions of the orbiting planets in order to *time* the appearance of those great magnetic storms we see in photographs, through a telescopic projection (or filtered lens) as small, dark blemishes. The false doctrine that it takes *centuries* for sunspots to appear is refuted by the fact that Nelson's forecasts are made months, weeks, sometimes only *days* before the appearance of sunspots—*not* centuries.

Then there is the really bad problem of the Sun's postulated neutrinos. These are elusive, weakly interacting, supposedly uncharged particles with no mass. Except for the fact that they've been generated by particle accelerators, this sounds like a good approximation of "nothing."

Being massless and chargeless, they virtually *never* interact with other particles. Neutrinos zip right out of the core and through the body of the Sun. Eight minutes later, they pass through the Earth and continue outward at the velocity of light. Because they are theoretically *supposed* to be born in the same nuclear reactions that cause the Sun to shine, scientists have set up some rather exotic experiments in attempts to determine what was happening when the invisible neutrinos "shone" right out of the Sun's core.

A mile deep in the Homestake Gold Mine near a South Dakota town with the unlikely name of Lead, physicist Raymond Davis and a group of colleagues from the Brookhaven National Laboratory set up an "observatory"—a 400,000-liter tank of perchloroethelyne (about the same stuff your local drycleaner uses)—in an attempt to detect even the tiniest reaction they could attribute to a neutrino.

Using "well-known physical laws" to put together a complete model of the Sun—with a computer to integrate all the differential equations from the Year One, physicists almost unanimously agree that neutrinos *must* be born in the solar core, where it gets as hot as 15 million degrees Centigrade and is one hundred times denser than "incompressible" water.

If there are no detectable neutrinos, then something is either terribly wrong with the Sun, or the solar physicists are all wet.

The crucial importance of the neutrino to astrophysics is the fact that it "interacts weakly." That's putting it mildly. According to scientific figures, a neutrino can penetrate *anything—and at light speed—* even a wall of solid lead more than 100 billion miles thick! (I gave up trying to figure out why those guys ever thought they could track a neutrino in a piddling tank of cleaning fluid.)

Margaret Silbar, in a science article in the February, 1977, issue of *Analog*, noting that no solar neutrinos could be traced, observed, "That's more than passing curious. Is something wrong with the Sun? We don't know yet." She suggested, as two alternatives, that "our physics must be changed drastically," or "the experiment is wrong," then concluded that to detect low-energy neutrinos, gallium should be substituted for chlorine. Unfortunately, gallium now costs more than $250 a pound and more than twenty tons of the stuff would be needed. No doubt they'll get the money from the Congressmen they've managed to scare half to death, as we'll soon see.

Even so, it would take years to set up the experiment. "It is only with new data that we will be able to sort the different possible ways out of the dilemma," said Ms. Silbar. "If even *low*-energy neutrinos are not being emitted from the solar furnace, something is very, *very* wrong with our Sun. Is it possible that our Sun will *not* peacefully continue evolving as a main-sequence star until it reaches the red giant stage? Maybe our Sun is not, after all, 'an ordinary star.'

"Perhaps the most frightening speculation along these lines," she concluded, "is that our Sun might have had an accident; it may have run into a quite small black hole in the very recent past,* which is sitting on the core, gobbling up mass from the surrounding gases and regurgitating energy. Radiation pressure keeps more than just a little bit of matter at a time from falling into the hole, but eventually, say, 150 million years, the Sun will be eaten up from within by this cancer. Nightmares, anyone?"

In the same issue of *Analog*, an article by British astrophysicist Dr. John Gribbin titled "Is Our Sun a Normal Star?" suggests: "If the geological record tells us, as it does, that the Sun has been hot for thousands of millions of years, but the absence of neutrinos now implies fusion is not going on as it should to keep the Sun hot for that long, the only satisfactory answer to my mind is that the Sun is not at present a 'normal' star—that it has gone 'off the boil' temporarily."

Whether the Sun's "flickering" changes in brightness (discovered late in 1975 by American astronomers) mean that it is in a seriously abnormal state caused by passing through galactic dust clouds, or is being gobbled up by a black hole in its gut seems irrelevant. Whichever may be true, damned few of us will be around to see it. Our remote descendants probably will have departed this system to resettle on planets orbiting younger, more stable main-sequence stars in another 10,000 or 20,000 years, perhaps a lot sooner.

It may have happened before—right here. It seems rather strange to me that only Caucasoid and Mongoloid humans are susceptible to skin cancer from over-

---

* This suggestion comes from D. D. Clayton of Rice University and his colleagues. According to this model, 51 percent of the Sun's luminosity comes from the black hole (which is about 10^{-5} of the solar mass), the rest from more conventional nuclear processes, which emit the equivalent of 1 SNU. (*Author's note*: 10^{-5} is about 100,000 times smaller than the Sun.)

exposure to sunlight at this distance from our local star. Black people aren't.

If the asteroid belt—that mass of rubble and debris orbiting between Mars and Jupiter where, according to Bode's Law, there should be a planet—does turn out to be a world destroyed either naturally or by its inhabitants, we could well be the descendants of the survivors of that holocaust.

A thorough investigation of the solar wind's interaction with the geomagnetic field and the complex cross-currents of the interplanetary force fields could form the basis of a new science such as that discovered by John H. Nelson. The ideas of the former RCA astro-weather forecaster are surprisingly similar to those of Nikola Tesla when that electrical genius tried to explain how his revolutionary polyphase power system worked.

"I have no solid theory to explain what I have observed," Nelson admitted. "But the similarity between an electric generator with its carefully placed magnets and the Sun with its ever-changing planets is intriguing. In the generator, the magnets are fixed and produce a constant electrical current. If we consider the planets as magnets and the Sun as the armature, we have a considerable similarity to the generator. However, in this case, the 'magnets' are *moving*. For this reason, the electromagnetic stability of the solar system varies widely."

Our star's *superspectrum* therefore undergoes cyclic changes, as does its light, coronal plasma and other radiations, often very irregularly. The scientific record of sunspot activity shows it to be somewhat erratic. The Sun's rotation during the so-called Maunder Minimum (when sunspots are very scarce) slows down and speeds up as much as 3 to 5 percent.

Our star's twenty-five-day rotation when observed from the viewpoint of the Earth, is twenty-seven days long. Moreover, it rotates at different speeds at different latitudes. The equatorial regions spin around considerably faster than the polar regions.

This solar rotation forms a magnetic dynamo that

generates a complicated magnetic field that, in combination with the angular positions of the orbiting planets and the center of gravity of the system, coincides with the appearances of sunspots that profoundly influence the geomagnetic field, the ion count of our atmosphere, the weather, and the biodynamic fields of every living thing on the planet. All life forms interact in physical and other still-mysterious ways. The terrestrial biosphere may itself be considered an invisible superorganism. The most complex individual physical organism known is the brain-body-mind of a human being. Similar to all living things, it is shaped and controlled by an individual electrodynamic field that seems to be a more basic (albeit mysterious) force in determining human health, longevity, and general vitality than the "giant molecule," DNA itself.

Since the whole *is* greater than its parts, the electrodynamic fields of life (or L-fields) may actually supercede the "authority" of the DNA's double-helix in shaping the physical organism. This rather heterodox concept violates the boundaries established by the physical sciences to isolate its functions from crackpot notions, nonphysical mysteries, and unfounded metaphysical theories.

Of course, physicists' belief in particles with characteristics such as "strangeness," "charm," or "psi," and the "reality" of invisible neutrinos that are totally without weight, have no effect on anything, can't *be* affected by anything, and whose passing cannot be detected by any known means as they zip from the solar core through the Earth, is "acceptable." In actual fact, though, it also seems to violate the basic tenets of the scientific method.

"The fairest thing we can experience," Albert Einstein once observed, "is the mysterious. It is the fundamental emotion which stands at the cradle of true art and science. He who knows it and can no longer wonder, no longer feel amazement, is as good as dead—a snuffed-out candle."

One of Einstein's chief collaborators, Dr. B.

Hoffman, in a joint statement with the Nobel laureate Pascal Jordan, said, *"A gravitational field has some similarity with the force which transmits telepathic information, in that both act at a distance and penetrate all obstacles."*

For ages, philosophers have pondered the phenomenon of thought, a product of mind—an ineffable force or energy that either employs the brain as transducer for the L-field, or vice-versa. In some mysterious way, therefore, the human field of life can be influenced by thought and demonstrably influenced by the electrochemical functions of the brain.

The electrodynamic fields of plant life were first detected by Dr. Andrew E. Douglass, founder of the science of dendrochronology, during his tenure at the University of Arizona. Dr. Douglass performed electrodynamic field tests on trees that he monitored continually for more than a decade. Electrodes were permanently embedded in the inner (still growing) layers of trees. The electromagnetic or L-fields of these trees reflected every change in heat, light, cold, atmospheric pressure—even storms and sunspots.

Closer studies revealed the staggering fact that the L-fields of the monitored trees *also* showed regular changes that were totally divorced from then-current environmental conditions. Dr. Douglass discovered that, through some mysterious method of plant "clairvoyance," the trees could anticipate in great detail events that actually occurred during the next forty-eight hours, including barometric changes, thunderstorms, and unexpected sunspots. The L-fields of the trees predicted the effect of atmospheric electricity in their cambia (inner layers) and produced graph tracings which read as though they were *currently* being stimulated.

According to Edward Russell in his book, *Design for Destiny*,* "In their present preoccupation with particles, biology and biochemistry are in the same stage that physics was years ago before 'particle

---

*London: Neville Spearman, 1971.

physics' gave place to 'field physics.' When biology finally matures and 'particle biology' gives way to *field biology* the role of genes and DNA will be seen in its true perspective."

The genial Mr. Russell makes a persuasive argument for the idea that neither genes nor DNA molecules have any power over the organism of which they are a part. The body, he points out, is far greater than the sum of its component parts—organs, cells, and molecules. The structure of molecules is so relatively simple in comparison to the whole organism that it is illogical—almost *inconceivable*—that DNA or any other molecule would have the power to control the entire body.

"These fields regulate and control all living things," said their discoverer, Dr. Harold S. Burr, after forty years of research at Yale University Medical School. "Though infinitely complicated, like other electromagnetic fields, they are influenced by the greater fields of the Universe. So man is an integral part of the Universe and shares in its purpose and destiny."

Dr. Burr's most brilliant and promising pupil, Dr. Leonard J. Ravitz, Jr., went on to discover that voltage measurements of the L-fields that control and maintain our physical organisms can be used to diagnose the condition not only of the body but also of the mind. Moreover, these electrodynamic fields seem to possess an even greater power of precognition than that of trees and other plants.

Only L-fields know the organism's need *in advance*, particularly while it is growing. Only L-fields are able to send the right molecular substances to the necessary part of the body *at the right time*. The genetic theory presumes that DNA and genes are the all-powerful matrices that replicate themselves through fission—by splitting apart. Actually, to function at all, such matrices *must* be independent of (and unaffected by) the material they allegedly mold.

Obviously DNA molecules are *not* independent of the body. In some unknown way, the electromagnetic properties of the L-field are profoundly different from EM as we now understand it. Moreover, the human L-field is more complex than those of trees, animals, or any other known form of life. In a study of 50,000 people since 1948 (at Yale, Duke, and the University of Pennsylvania Schools of Medicine), the L-field readings revealed subjective changes in feeling, emotion, and behavior that were completely beyond the detection capabilities of any other method.

"To ignore the study of the overriding L-field in favor of some anthropomorphic gene or DNA molecule," said Edward Russell, "is unproven supposition—perhaps 'superstition' would be more accurate."

Although Dr. S. E. Luria, MIT's Nobel laureate in physiology, skirts the issue of "vitalism," i.e., the theory that once explained the uniqueness of living organisms by postulating a "vital force," the metaphysical idea that each organism has a vital soul imposed upon it from outside, he observed that genetics doesn't deal with statistical averages but with "the deterministic, exact maintenance of all the millions of different genes in every cell . . . this is accomplished by a rigid system which enforces the entry of just one copy of each gene into each germ cell and the exact duplication of each gene whenever a cell divides. *This mechanism requires a degree of order, or organized information, that is found nowhere else in Nature, not even in the movement of the planets.*

"It is a key feature of life to achieve the maintenance of a high degree of order in the face of the physical tendency of all organized systems to undergo increasing thermodynamic disorder."

The film *Star Wars* popularized the concept of "the Force" as a kind of universal constant. Just as it is with the L-field, there was no entropy, so the Force was *beyond* the spectral range of electromagnetic radiation. Individually as well as collectively, the human L-field interacts with those of every other living thing on the planet (and I suspect, throughout the physical Universe). If this seems to be "vitalism," so be it (and may the Force be with you). We are all integral parts of the solar superspectrum, and electricity (or a similar, although more refined and subtle kind of energy) seems to control the direction of the entire terrestrial biosphere and, therefore, controls human destiny. Within the broad parameters of this path, humans do seem to have greater relative freedom of choice than any other family, genera, or species.

Since the *élan vital*, the Force, the Essence, the L-field, or whatever name we choose for it, *is* part of the solar superspectrum, our understanding of electromagnetic behavior should be a good clue. Massive electromagnetic storms on the Sun often generate more electrical power than the entire civilized world, at its present stage of development, could consume in several million years.

The word electricity comes from *elektron*, the Greek word for amber, which was known by the Egyptians and Greeks to attract objects and generate sparks (of static electricity) when it was rubbed with wool. Magnetism is named for Magnesia, the Greek coastal area on the Aegean Sea where the first permanent magnets, called *"magnes,"* are *supposed* to have been discovered about 3,000 years ago. Because magnets were used by early mariners to navigate, they were also called lodestones, after the lodestar (or guiding star). That, at any rate, is the standard scientific explanation of man's earliest knowledge of electricity. Again, the established orthodox system conveniently ignores, rejects, or suppresses any sufficiently annoying idea, particularly when it threatens to upset its carefully nurtured version of how things ought to be. The Chinese, for example, are known to have used magnetic compasses as long ago as 2700 B.C. This is a fairly well-kept secret insofar as most students of electrical engineering are concerned, as are facts about Nikola Tesla's astounding feats, which qualify him as the greatest of all electrical geniuses (as you will discover in the next chapter).

Now that you are aware of the *standard* version of the origin of electrical knowledge, consider the following. In 1938, Dr. Wilhelm Konig, who was working in the national museum in Iraq, found the remnants of dry-cell electric batteries in a small tower which formed part of a Parthian settlement at a place called Khujut Rabu. The amazed German archaeologist soon discovered that four similar objects had been found at Seleucia, a few miles downriver.

When he returned to Germany, Dr. Konig searched a museum in Berlin and found ten more dry cells virtually identical to the one from his original dig, but they had been broken down into their component parts (as if someone had been interrupted before being able to assemble the pieces into working batteries).

Willard F. M. Gray of the General Electric High Voltage Laboratory in Pittsfield, Massachusetts, learned about the discovery and immediately volunteered to make an exact duplicate of the Parthian battery. Dr. Willy Ley, one of the most respected scientists of his time (who later became famous for his books on astronomy, rocketry, and planetary exploration in America), provided a complete metallurgical analysis of the "Baghdad Batteries," with precise dimensions and diagrams.

It was, of course, impossible to know what the Parthians used as the original electrolyte (it might have been acetic or citric acid, with which the Parthians were familiar, or something totally unknown, perhaps stronger than anything we have today). Lacking this information, Willard Gray used copper sulfate and found it worked perfectly. As of 1960, the battery was on display at the Berkshire Museum at Pittsfield, Massachusetts, and may still be there.

Unless the Parthians had a more efficient electrolyte, the five-inch-long battery, which was an inch-and-a-half in diameter, probably had an output of two volts per cell. The ancients had soldered the sheet-copper cylinder's edges with a 60/40 lead–tin alloy. This compares favorably with the best modern batteries. A copper disc had been crimped into the bottom of the cylinder and a layer of pitch or bitumen insulated it from the electrode; an iron rod in an asphalt stopper had been shoved into the top of the copper cylinder.

The irony is that the Baghdad Batteries are completely accepted as being just what they are. What they were used *for* is a total mystery. Yet there's great reluctance among orthodox scientists to admit that electrical batteries were being used 3,000 years ago. (You can usually predict what position a man will take if you know what position he holds.)

In 600 B.C., Thales of Miletus, who was renowned in his own time as a formidable scientist, astrologer, mathematician, and statesman (he predicted the eclipse of May 28, 585 B.C., and several earthquakes), knew about electricity, magnetism, and the processes used in manufacturing batteries (see *Encyclopaedia Britannica*, 1948, Vol. 17, pp. 344-345).

In a chapter appropriately titled "Frightfully Ancient Electrics," in his extraordinary book, *Investigating the Unexplained* (Englewood Cliffs, N. J.: Prentice-Hall, 1972), the late Ivan E. Sanderson, one of the most erudite, prolific writers, as well as witty and charming of men, wrote, "It would seem that the generation of electrical current by friction is more than just implied in several of the even more ancient Veddic Indian writings. (Back to the mercury engines that were said to power some of the *vimanas*.)"

Sanderson reported in some detail about the discovery by Egyptologists Mariette and Chassinat in 1939, of a bas-relief from the Temple of Hathor at Dendera "which obviously shows electric lamps held up by high-tension insulators. . . . The Old World, and notably the Near East," he said, "is liberally littered with evidence of the use of electrical power by the ancients, and not only in the form of things such as we call 'Leyden jars,' but also of really large and potentially powerful generators."

Like John Nelson and Nikola Tesla, Sanderson, too, suggested that the Ark of the Covenant was a powerful electric condenser and radio broadcasting and receiving apparatus through which "God" spoke to Moses *after* giving him very specific instructions for building the Ark. The Ark was made of shittim (setim) wood and lined with gold inside and out, the exact principle of an electric condenser: two conductors separated by insulation with a gold crown around it. (See *Exodus*, Chapter 25).

As a prince of Egypt, Moses may have learned many scientific secrets from the priests of the Temple. If they had such knowledge of electricity, it was lost until 1802 when an Italian lawyer, Grandomenico Romagnosi, discovered quite by accident that an electric current flowing through a wire will deflect a magnetic needle in its vicinity, thereby founding the new science of electromagnetics.

Thus ended the hoary Dark Age mechanistic theory of matter, and the age of electricity was born. Michael Faraday discovered in 1831 that a moving magnet, conversely, will induce an electric current to flow in a wire. This integration of electricity with magnetism, with its pervasive concept of *continuous fields* of energy—of "forces acting at a distance"—was interpreted by Faraday and by James Clerk Maxwell as a definable region extending through space and having detectable influences.

Electromagnetism and gravity are propagated at light speed and permeate space in all directions from the Sun, but are subject to attenuation by the inverse-square law and (except for gravity) can be shielded, isolated, and directed. The L-field also has these characteristics and seems to have its (non-entropic) origin somewhere beyond the spectral range of electromagnetic radiation. Moreover, there are far too many historical incidents of null gravity to be ignored by science.

During the many ingenious experiments of Joseph Henry, Michael Faraday, and James Clerk Maxwell, the working differences between electricity and magnetism were clearly demonstrated. There was a remarkable contrast in the field orientations. Lines of electricity, for instance, form a field that is always *perpendicular* to the surfaces of conductors (i.e., tubes or wires). Lines of magnetic force, conversely, always form fields that are parallel to magnetic surfaces.

In the second volume of Guy Murchee's *Music of the Spheres* (Boston: Houghton Mifflin, 1961; New York: Dover, 1967), the author draws astronomical analogies between the contrary action of gravity and electromagnetism: "Such rather mysterious yet graceful correlations illuminating the warp and woof of the electromagnetic tapestry were eventually compiled, along with all other experimental data, into laws governing basic electrical and magnetic behavior which the mathematical genius of Maxwell found a way to express in four beautiful relations—which have served as the cornerstone of electromagnetic theory ever since."

Inevitably, electromagnetism was used more and more in the physicist's search for the "ultimate particle." Equally inevitably, research has been conducted in the ephemeral area of the effect of nonphysical forces on human thought. Telepathy is a real phenomenon (as astronaut Edgar Mitchell proved in telepathic experiments during his return voyage from the Moon); it is not impeded by distance, seems to have no connection with electromagnetic radiation, is not influenced by gravity, and cannot be explained by physics.

The electrodynamic fields of life are, as we have seen, superceded by a vastly superior field, of which the solar *superspectrum* is an instrument. In *Design for Destiny*, Edward Russell calls this power "the Essence."

Our civilization, having achieved almost total global communication, still must have many built-in safeguards against possible error. Our system is not infallible. Here is Mr. Russell's remarkable analogy between modern communications, the organization of the Universe, and the powers of the Essence:

> As an organization, the Universe is not only inconceivably immense and complex, but also fantastically dynamic. Everything in it, from parti-

cles to galaxies, is in a constant state of motion and change. It is not—as some still seem to think—a machine which can run on its own because machines do not change their components as the Universe does. Stars explode and cool off, radiation varies, comets and meteorites race through space, magnetic fields and climates change, different forms of life appear and disappear. And, to make things more difficult, we—and probably other beings elsewhere—have been given some free will and the power to disrupt the organization. In short, the Universe is an organizer's nightmare.

Yet it has been running smoothly for many billions of years and, despite all the changes, the balance of Nature is maintained. Our experience of human organization suggests that this would not have been possible without faultless instantaneous "telecommunications" within the system—without an omniscient awareness of every detail and event. Otherwise there would have been chaos long ago.

Since relatively simple human organizations can be damaged by minor errors or neglected details, we can assume that the intricate, interdependent organization of the Universe cannot tolerate the smallest piece of *unexpected* grit in the machine. The organization cannot permit any accidents, even if it sometimes seems to us that it does. As someone put it: "Man's accidents are God's purposes."

As the Essence is pure Mind and the Universe the product of Its thoughts, Its awareness of events in any part of the Universe must be by means of what we can picture as "a radar of thought." This must function instantaneously because we can hardly imagine that the Essence can be kept waiting for information, even for a small fraction of a microsecond.

So vast a Universe, in which everything moves at enormous speeds could not operate if the thoughts of its Organizer were weakened by distance or subject to any delay in transmission—the Universe cannot be measured in "thought-years." This need not surprise us because speed is a property of time and distance a property of space. As both time and space are products of the Mind of the Essence we would expect thought to be entirely independent of them.

Russell's conclusion here parallels that of Sir James Jeans, who suggested that the Universe consists of the thought of a mathematical thinker. I find this a bit too cold and abstract, however. Moreover, it is in direct contradiction to some of the historical facts and their congruent legends which you will find in the final pages of this book.

"Thoughts generated by human minds," says Russell, "just have properties similar to those of the Essence because human minds are particles of the Essence. When human thoughts are transmitted, therefore, they must use some channel—so to speak—of the telecommunications of the Universe. So it is not surprising that nobody—as far as the writer knows—has ever found that human thought-transmission is either weakened by distance or restricted to the speed of light, which physicists assume to be the ultimate speed of the Universe. Thought is faster—it is instantaneous."

Since our brains are transducers of the L-field, it would seem prudent to take a closer look at electromagnetism and electricity—as part of this field—and the real story of Nikola Tesla, a strange electrical genius who dedicated his life to the technological and spiritual betterment of his terrestrial family.

CHAPTER 6
Tesla Electrifies the Earth

There are those people who believe that Nikola Tesla was from another world. Certainly he was one of the strangest figures in scientific history. Tesla possessed supersensitive sight and hearing, and was often distracted by his weird ability to "feel" through his skin. He also had an acute sense of precognition which enabled him to "see" *all the hundreds of moving parts and thousands of precision-tooled components* of the polyphase alternating-current power system with which he would revolutionize world civilization. He was tortured by radar-sensitivity and—like a bat—could often detect objects in total darkness.

Although he was a "hard" scientist and had the finest education available, the aristocratic electrical genius was a first-rate troubleshooter who could perform shirt-sleeve miracles repairing any existing power system breakdown. Yet he was also "superstitious" about numbers and had a strange belief that the Sun and Earth were dynamic living things.

Tesla was born during a severe electrical storm on July 10, 1856, in the Austro-Hungarian hamlet of Smiljan, now part of Yugoslavia; he died, an American citizen, but a lonely, eccentric recluse, on January 7, 1943, in his room on the thiry-third floor of the New Yorker Hotel. His funeral was marred by a conflict between the Serbians and the Utashi (Croatian Nationalists striving to separate from Yugoslavia). At his death, accolades poured in from all over the world from the high and the mighty, many of whom had become extremely wealthy because of the inventor's patented works.

During his lifetime, Tesla was honored by an entire spectrum of humanity—from King Peter II of Yugoslavia to the late Marshal Josip Broz (Tito). When he died, Franklin and Eleanor Roosevelt were among the first to express their sorrow and their gratitude. Single-handedly, Tesla probably contributed as much to the advancement of modern science and technology as Marconi, Heinrich Hertz, John Clerk Maxwell, Charles Steinmetz, Alexander Graham Bell, and Thomas Edison combined.

His patents have made billions in profits for others, yet at his death Tesla's entire estate was less than $2,000, a paltry sum for a man who, at the request of George Westinghouse, once tore up a contract worth more than $12 million in order to save the Westinghouse Electric Company from bankruptcy. (Years later, before sailing off on a luxury cruise to Europe, Westinghouse bluntly rejected the once-proud Tesla's humble plea for a $5,000 loan.)

Considering his circumstances at the end of his life, it seemed ironic that Tesla had ever been feted by European royalty at the peak of his dazzling career. Among his admirers were conductor Ignace Paderewski, author Rudyard Kipling, J. Pierpont Morgan and John Jacob Astor (the two richest men in the world), George Westinghouse, the pioneering science-fiction publisher Hugo Gernsbach, and scores of prominent scientists, inventors, politicians, and industrialists—as well as the most beautiful young women of his time (another irony for a man who was by nature, choice, and temperament a complete celibate). His friend Mark Twain occasionally visited his laboratories and was astounded by the inventor's genius.

His life was marked by almost unbelievable changes in fortune. He arrived in America in 1884, a tall, gaunt young immigrant with only four cents in his pocket (he had been robbed), a book of his own poems, a package of detailed plans for a flying machine, and a letter of introduction to Thomas Edison.

Although Tesla was the most important electrical genius of the nineteenth and twentieth centuries, to this day an astonishing number of students manage to finish formal engineering educations without ever having heard of him; if he is remembered at all it is as the somewhat obscure inventor of something called the Tesla coil. In death, as in life, Edison continues to overshadow the reputation of the enigmatic Slav.

Yet long before the turn of the century, Tesla conceived ultrasound and laserlike death rays and guided missiles. He designed a jet-propelled automobile that could travel on land, water, or through the air—even electrical propulsion engines for interplanetary voyages. He regarded the Sun as a vital living entity whose rotating magnetic fields would provide all of mankind's energy needs for scores of thousands of years. The shy, intense immigrant also seemed to have had the strange power of "seeing" into the future. The polyphase alternating current system came to him in one overwhelming flash of illumination in 1879 while he was watching a sunset in a Budapest park.

By 1890 American industry had begun to build on the weak, inefficient, and costly direct power systems developed and largely controlled by Thomas Edison, who eventually tried to prohibit the use of Tesla's patented polyphase system. In spite of all obstacles, the first Tesla alternating current system was installed at Niagara Falls in 1895–1896 (three 5,000-horsepower generators); it is still operating, producing exactly the same kind of current as modern atomic energy plants.

Before Roentgen discovered X-rays, Tesla had taken "shadowgraph" pictures of the inside of the human body. He anticipated and discovered radar and sonar. He designed, built, and demonstrated remote-controlled boats and submarines before Marconi was unfairly credited with sending the first trans-Atlantic radio message—the letter "s." (The patent decision was eventually reversed by the Supreme Court in Tesla's favor.)

Although it now seems more like a science-fiction story from one of Hugo Gernsbach's early pulp magazines, the ascetic electrical wizard conceived and patented more than 800 inventions—many of which were a century or more ahead of their time. Even now, some are being developed secretly, others are still considered either impractical or too advanced.

If we ever erased the results of Tesla's patents, modern industry and technology would come to a dead halt. We would still be struggling along on steam power and direct current that could not be transmitted more than a few miles. Tesla's contributions embrace the whole field of constant speed synchronous, induction, and split-phase motors, and are so complete that there have been no basic changes whatever since the introduction of his discoveries. Moreover, in the long history of litigation and legal battles over the rights covered in Tesla's patents, not a single claimant has ever been successful.

In the field of radio transmission alone, Tesla's papers and lectures—especially before the Royal Institution in England—proved how far-reaching his ideas were. They covered the basic elements of antenna and ground circuits coupled with transmission and receiving circuits tuned to the same frequency. Neither Lodge nor Popov nor Slaby nor Marconi conceived or used an aerial conductor or ground connection until 1897 when they achieved radio transmission. By then, Tesla had discovered that live television pictures could be sent along wires or through the atmosphere.

He had the disconcerting habit of visualizing developments centuries in the future, and his work was so advanced that even today Soviet scientists are still trying to unravel and employ the results of his pioneering work. Early in 1977, for example, the United States and western Europe were alarmed by a series of unprecedented "blasts" from a strange, powerful transmitter based in the Soviet Union. It drowned out the Voice of America and all European and American broadcasts.

Diplomatic complaints were soon followed by intelligence reports that Soviet scientists and agents had been at work in the Tesla Museum in Belgrade, translating many of the long-forgotten diaries of the electrical genius. Since then, electronic eavesdropping by Russian agents and the deleterious effects of invisible microwaves on American diplomatic personnel in the Soviet capital have baffled Westerners in the Soviet Union. It is now estimated that nearly 200 of Tesla's patented inventions remain untouched and undeveloped.

Many of the inventor's fondest dreams were thwarted, sometimes suppressed. The one with greatest potential was a system of transmitting electrical power without wires—through the atmosphere and even the Earth itself. For a time, the project was supported by J. Pierpont Morgan, who eventually pulled the financial rug from under it. Later, Tesla's huge transmitting tower on Long Island was destroyed by the U.S. government—on the pretext that it was being used to signal German submarines.

The story was, of course, apocryphal. Tesla's worldwide wireless superpower system was destroyed at the behest of the financial wizards when the awful truth was learned: not a nickel of profit could be turned on electricity that could be generated inexpensively and then transmitted as freely as the air we breathe.

One of the Hearst chain's chief editorial writers, Arthur Brisbane, once joined Tesla at his favorite restaurant, Delmonico's, for an interview that later appeared in the New York *World*. It was dawn before the two men had finished talking, and Delmonico's scrub women were arriving.

During the all-night interview, new worlds were opened to the amazed reporter. When he was told about the superior, less expensive fluorescent light, Brisbane wrote: "Compared with Tesla's light, Edison's incandescent lamp is as primitive as an oxcart with two solid wooden wheels compared to modern railroading." The scientist told his guest that the mystery of the transmission of life-giving light from the Sun was the result of vibrations—a staggering figure of *500 trillion* vibrations a second—through space. "All I have to do to duplicate sunlight is to get this number of vibrations to the second with my machinery ... I have succeeded to a certain point and am still at work on it," Tesla said.

The reporter later wrote about some of "the electrician's" laboratory demonstrations in which "he came out of his experiments a most radiant creature, with light flaming at every pore of his skin and from the tips of his fingers and from every hair on his head."

But Brisbane couldn't conceive of anything approaching 500 trillion vibrations, and said so.

"Look my friend," Tesla tried to explain, "if a mass of metal as big as the Delmonico Restaurant, in which we sat, had ten thousand times the resisting force of the most finely tempered steel and could be made to vibrate with one millionth of the rapidity of light-producing electric vibrations in space, that mass of metal, ten thousand times harder than steel, would simply vanish into air like smoke. It would disappear into atoms too small to be seen."

The newspaperman was amazed by the enormous power of electricity and wanted to know how much it weighed. Tesla laughed. "Absolutely nothing. As you've already seen, I can easily prove it; I will load you so full of electricity without harm, so much that you can't hold any more, and then put you on the finest weighing machine, and you will not find one-thousandth part of an ounce added to your weight."

They discussed the force magnets must exert to hold a piece of iron perfectly still. Such power is wasted, Tesla told him, adding that he could get a magnet to use its force so as to make a piece of iron spin violently around and around. Moreover, he could also make a wheel at some distance from the source of electromagnetic force spin around—*with 10,000 horsepower*—exactly what he designed as the basic principle in his plans for the Niagara Falls power station.

"We are all whirling through endless space," the inventor explained in 1895, "with an inconceivable speed, all around us everything is spinning, everything is moving. We will tap this inexhaustible store of energy. With the light of the Sun and the power derived from it . . . obtained without effort . . . humanity will advance with giant strides. I have produced electrical discharges more than a hundred feet long; but it would not be difficult to reach lengths one hundred times as great . . . I have produced electrical movements of approximately one hundred thousand horsepower, but rates of one million or ten million horsepower are easily practicable."

He was as good as his word. Using a secret magnifying transmitter to reproduce one of Nature's rarest and most terrifying phenomena, he succeeded in creating ball lightning at his laboratory in Colorado Springs in 1899, a feat that has not been duplicated today. (As we'll see in a later chapter, thirty to fifty years later professional physicists were still denying the existence or reality of ball lightning.)

In 1977, in the vast, empty hangar where the first atomic bomb was assembled, Dr. Robert K. Golka and Robert W. Bass attempted to repeat the experiment (based on Tesla's unpublished notes), allegedly with "the highest voltages ever produced by man" up to that time—20 million volts (more later about this claim). It was called Project Tesla, an attempt to create fusion power—the very same energy source Tesla recognized as being generated within the Sun and stars.

Physicist James Tuck, who founded the American fusion program, is convinced that the lightning ball holds the key to fantastically cheap and endless energy for man's future on this planet. The fuel is deuterium or "heavy water," which can be extracted inexpensively from the oceans to provide millions of years of power.

No one knows exactly how Tesla built his magnifying transmitter to create ball lightning almost a century ago. But the situation hampers fusion research and has been full of unpleasant surprises for scientists experimenting with laser implosions, magnetic confinement, and unexpected electrical explosion.

Ball lightning is believed to be a plasma—sometimes red, orange, or yellow, sometimes blue. It frequently appears during lightning storms, and sometimes, mysteriously, when it is clear and calm. The ball often floats around, even against the strongest winds; sometimes it comes through a glass window or a closed screen—with or without damage! (The author's Maine home was once the site of a weird experience, according to previous tenants who heard a sizzling, crackling sound at the screened kitchen door, and watched, frozen with fear in the living room as the yellow-white ball of lightning bounced through the house, making four right- and three left-angle turns through the rooms, then exited through the screened front porch door. Circular holes about fifteen inches in diameter were burned through both screens.)

There are reports of ball lightning materializing inside or even outside aircraft in flight, with no deformation whatever from winds in excess of 300 miles per hour. Dean Acheson when he was Secretary of State, reported seeing one across the breakfast table aboard the President's plane. In one building at Hill Air Force Missile Radiographic Facility, in Utah, about once a year, volleyball-size fireballs drop mysteriously right out of empty air next to the high voltage supply of the twenty-five-megavolt linear accelerator. Usually it's a ball of blue fire that floats to the floor, rolls gently or bounces, and then rises to the power supply area where it just dissipates its energy with no apparent damage to anything. Not even the most expert troubleshooters can find an explanation for the repetitions of the phenomena. Lightning once struck the large concrete building, which has a sixty-foot ceiling inside. In the same instant, a baseball-sized sphere of intense fire formed over the conduit on the wall four feet above ground and floated along the wall for about thirty feet. Then it did something utterly baffling: the fireball floated away from the wall, swung around the neck and shoulders of a man standing absolutely motionless near the wall, then moved back and continued along the wall for another meter or so until it came to a double outlet on the conduit. There it exploded, blowing the electrical system of the entire building.

Although fireballs are believed to be plasmoids, they present utterly baffling problems to the presently known laws of physics because their stability and bouncing indicate that they have very strong surface tension, which plasmoids are not known to possess. By any definition, fireballs represent a profound scientific mystery in that they seem to be a totally unknown state of matter. To make things worse for the scientists, no presently known laws can account for the *propulsion* of the fireballs. According to *Design News* (April 20, 1976), Project Tesla had developed a stringent mathematical model of the lightning ball's absolute asymptotic, fluid-dynamical stability. Early computer analyses indicated extreme density (10^{13}-10^{11} cm^{-3}) and a temperature seven times hotter than the Sun!

Many of Tesla's statements, particularly during his later years when he tried so desperately to carry his work further than any financier would allow, were considered "extravagant." One of these was his persistent belief that the Sun was charged with energies beyond the ability of man or his instruments to measure, and that myriad energies, radiating most intensely from the solar equatorial region, had enormous impact on life on Venus, Earth, Mars, and Jupiter. He was convinced that life existed everywhere—often in forms almost impossible to recognize. He believed that two or more global civilizations like our own could exist in the same space at the same time. "Intelligent beings exist on other planets in a form unknown to us. We cannot positively say that some of them might not be present here, in this our world, in the very midst of us, for their constitution and life manifestation may be such that we are unable to perceive them."

His other statements, many of which were misquoted, misunderstood, or distorted, coupled with his eccentricities, intense creativity, and power of concentration, often made him appear to be a luminous-eyed creature from another world. Tesla's iconoclasm was eventually used as an excuse to destroy his reputation as a credible scientist. Although his enemies admitted that he gave the world an entire system of alternating-current power transmission, mechanisms for industrial induction heating and welding, medical diathermy units, synchronous time devices, fluorescent and neon gaseous tube lighting, and the whole groundwork for radio and other systems of communication, they ridiculed his weird visions, hallucinations, and the strange compulsions that afflicted him so cruelly.

His friends tried to find reasons: "Nikola's visions may be caused by some physical deviation of the optic nerve or by peculiar brain structure," said one young woman whom he often wined and dined at Delmonico's (always with proper Victorian courtesy and courtliness; Tesla placed all women on the proverbial pedestal—safely beyond emotional reach).

According to Inez Hunt and Wanetta Draper in their book, *Lightning in His Hands*, "He took no chances on any physical or emotional contact. Even the divine Sarah Bernhardt, who coyly dropped her handkerchief one time near his café table in Paris, failed to arouse more than courtesy in Tesla, who sprang to his feet to retrieve the bit of lace, avoided her eyes as he returned it, and immediately resumed his conversation with a friend about wireless telegraphy."

Such behavior probably seems ridiculous to the world today. But Tesla was always very courteous and considerate of the women who worked in his office. "If they were asked to work overtime," wrote the Mss. Hunt and Draper, "Tesla saw that they had a good dinner at Delmonico's and that they were transported by cab. He, himself, never rode with them, but followed at a distance in another cab—and always picked up the tab."

Oddly enough, he had pretty definite ideas about

fashion and women's appearance. "He believed that the lines of a woman's dress should follow the lines of Nature and not Paris dictates," said Hunt and Draper. "At one time when his secretary appeared in a high style dress with a waist far below the normal line, Tesla considerately sent her home in a cab to change before anyone saw her in what he considered a monstrosity. He believed that women should not marry too young, 'for then,' he said, 'men marry you for your beauty.'

"Nevertheless, he liked beautiful women and enjoyed the company of intellectual ones, but he always reserved the privilege of completely de-sexing them in his mind."

The inventor's strange vanity seemed assuaged by the admiration of women with whom he could communicate. He liked to impress them with his plans to send messages *through* the Earth without wires, or to transmit electricity without waste. He enjoyed dazzling them with tales of his experiments and ideas. After explaining the difference between voltage and amperage, he would tell a female dinner guest that by using low amperage, he could put a million volts of electricity safely through his body—and he often demonstrated it to the thrilled (or terrified) young lady.

In those horse-and-buggy days Tesla predicted the age of automation and enjoyed the prospect of easing the workload of humanity. "The day will come when most of our daily tasks will be done simply by pressing buttons," he said one evening. Then he fell into a thoughtful silence and mused, "Hard work never killed anyone, but excessive play could. As for love and marriage," he smiled, "they would simply interfere with the success of my work."

When he was en route to the ship that was to take him to the United States, he was robbed of his luggage, tickets, and all his money. Nevertheless, he remembered the exact number of his steamship ticket and was finally allowed to make the journey to New

York when the thief failed to arrive to claim the reservation.

Although he was always a gentleman, Tesla was a formidable foe in a fight, as the crew of the ship that took him to America learned when young Tesla took their side in a near mutiny against a cruel, tyrannical complement of ship's officers.

When he arrived virtually penniless in America, the young inventor, whose view of the rotating Sun from Budapest had triggered the vision that would change the world, was broke and depressed. Instead of a land of dreams, America's bleak reality came as something of a shock.

In his eyes, America was a century behind Europe in civilization. Because he didn't even have enough money for carfare to reach a friend who was living in New York, he started to walk. Tired and hungry long before he reached his destination, Tesla passed a shoe repair shop, looked in the window, and noticed that the owner was trying to fix his electrical stitching-and-trimming machine. The motor was about the only familiar thing Tesla had seen in this strange land, so he simply walked into the shop. The disgusted shoemaker, who was about ready to give up, eagerly accepted the young Slav's offer of help. In less than two hours the electric motor and the machine were as good as new, and the grateful shoemaker handed the surprised Tesla twenty dollars for his trouble.

With that princely sum, he enjoyed a good lunch before presenting himself and his letter of introduction from Charles Batchellor, the manager of the Edison plant in Paris, to Thomas Edison. On the basis of Tesla's brilliant performance in Budapest, Strasbourg, and Paris, Batchellor had urged the young engineer to go to America and redesign Edison's machines. "I know two great men," the genial, bearded Englishman had written to Edison, "and you are one of them; the other is this young man."

Edison was not impressed.

But Tesla was. "This wonderful man who, without early advantage and scientific training, has accomplished so much," he later said in awe. Actually they had little in common. Aside from the fact that both were prodigious readers, they were worlds apart in character, temperament, and creative ability. Tesla was fluent in a dozen languages, he knew and appreciated literature, art, and music, and he seemed just too damned proper and aristocratic for the earthy, temperamental Edison's taste.

It wasn't long before the immigrant perceived an unexpectedly coarse streak in Thomas Alva Edison's character. The older man sized up the light-eyed applicant with barely concealed resentment. He hired him, but it was clear from the outset that he was suspicious of Tesla's cultured mannerisms, his impressive scholastic achievements and talents, and mainly the Serbian's enthusiasm for his alternating current motor which Tesla, with eager innocence, offered to share with Edison.

The American was dour. "My plant is doing just fine as it is," he said to the upstart. "It doesn't need any improvements."

Almost as though he was punishing him, Edison gave Tesla the job of doing minor routine jobs around the plant—mostly the dirty work of repairing burned-out armatures and broken-down dynamos, the very hallmarks of the stubborn Edison's direct current system.

Within months, word of Tesla's incredible ideas spread, and reached the ears of J. Pierpont Morgan, who eventually helped finance the Tesla Electric Company, where the inventor's staggering vision of rotating magnetic fields, experienced while looking at the Sun in Budapest, was translated into reality—right down to die-cut and small machine-tooled parts with tolerances of less than one ten-thousandth of an inch. Not a single component of the alternating current system had ever been tested except in the inventor's mind, where it had been kept alive and running for years without a single failure or breakdown. Tesla's memory was more holographic than photographic. Keeping the alternating current system, with all its parts, operating in the back of his mind during those years in which he developed hundreds of other ideas, was a prodigious feat.

The robust, mercurial Edison's temperament frequently shifted from laughter to anger, and he often exhibited a somewhat sadistic sense of humor. Once, out of sheer admiration, Tesla asked the older man where he got his phenomenal energy. "I eat Welsh rabbit for breakfast every single day of my life," Edison said with a straight face. He knew all about his assistant's sparse appetite and sensitive stomach. Naturally, Tesla came into work the next few days looking like a sick dog, and Edison roared with laughter at the "dumb bohunk."

(Edison neither knew nor cared anything about Tesla's background, or where he was born. "Bohunk," initially used to refer to Slavs or gypsies, and later to Poles, was eventually shortened to "hunky," an alternate ethnic reference to replace "Polack." This is the real origin of the sobriquet "honky," the current fanciful reference to Caucasians. It should be obvious to everyone by now that we are all *Terrans*.)

Paradoxically, although he frequently referred to the enigmatic "bohunk" as a *Parisian*, Edison simply took it for granted that Tesla originated in some terribly uncivilized part of the world. He once shocked his young assistant by asking with perfect sincerity whether he had ever eaten human flesh.

Tesla concealed his dislike for Edison's direct current motors but worked hard to improve the performance of the dynamos. He knew he could increase their output, lower their cost, and decrease the expensive maintenance, and he told his boss about it. Edison was interested. "Is that so?" he said brightly. "If you can do that, young fellow, it will be worth fifty thousand dollars to you." Tesla could hardly believe his ears. In those days $50,000 was all he needed for an entire lifetime of scientific exploration, the realization of his life's dream: having his own laboratory and workshop. So he plunged into work and drove himself harder than ever, going without food or rest for days at a time—exceeding his own endurance. He succeeded in designing twenty-four different kinds of standard machines, short cores, and uniform patterns to replace the outmoded hardware his employer was using.

Edison was overjoyed. Tesla waited patiently for the $50,000, which failed to appear in his pay envelope. Finally he came right out and asked for the promised bonus. Edison looked at his gaunt, exhausted employee in utter astonishment. "Hell, Tesla," he said, "you just don't understand American humor. I didn't really *mean* that I would give you fifty thousand dollars."

Tesla's faith was shattered. The long, grueling months of hard labor had sapped his health, he was sick with disillusion and disappointment. He tried to say something, but the words turned to dust and ashes in his mouth. Somehow, he managed to turn in his resignation. Tesla must have hated Edison intensely at the moment, but good breeding prevented him from expressing it. He was a gentleman, and gentlemen always behaved properly. One witness said, "He actually tipped his hat to Edison as he left the laboratory."

Shortly thereafter, Tesla was in business for himself, designing the dynamos, motors, transformers, and other devices for his soon-to-be-famous polyphase power system. Thomas Edison, the robust, hard-driving genius whose direct current system was constantly plagued by breakdowns and failures, may have regretted his cruelty and emotional outbursts.

Meanwhile, Tesla's plans soon intrigued the president of the Westinghouse Electric Company in Pittsburgh. George Westinghouse offered Tesla a cool million dollars for his patents on all phases of the alternating current system. Although he wasn't what you could call a shrewd businessman, the Serbian inventor held out for—and received—an additional royalty of one dollar per horsepower.

Tesla's system at Niagara Falls was a smashing success. The irony was that it also made it possible for Edison's incandescent lamp to operate efficiently instead of constantly burning out as it had because of his unstable direct current system.

During that era of *laissez faire* economics it was inevitable that sooner or later a power war would be waged among the giants of electricity. During the long battle between General Electric and Westinghouse, a series of mergers brought George Westinghouse to the brink of financial disaster. He visited Tesla's office and begged to be released from the one-dollar-per-horsepower royalty clause; by then, Westinghouse owed Tesla $12 million.

"To pay such an amount now would ruin me," he said. "I'd be finished and so would my company." Tesla rose without a word, walked to his file, pulled out the contract, and tore it up.

"It's more important for people to have alernating current," he said quietly, "than it is for me to have twelve million dollars."

With his polyphase system now secure, Tesla went to work on the wireless transmission of power. He was sure that no one had discovered all of Nature's electrical secrets, and he believed just as strongly that electricity wasn't an end but just a result of the Earth's natural magnetic vibrations, which were caused by the rotating electromagnetic fields of the Sun. He believed it was possible to use electricity to produce magnetic waves with which he could then distribute energy without wires. At his Colorado laboratory he had developed the famous Tesla Coil, and produced millions of high-frequency volts.

He must have been a strange, almost ghostly figure, working alone in his Colorado laboratory in the weirdly flickering light of the electrical discharges. Night and day he wore two-inch-thick insulated soles and a white laboratory coat. Tesla often expressed what must have seemed incomprehensible, if not totally insane ideas for 1899. He deplored man's inadequate conception of life, including his own. Even a crystal was a form of life, he declared, and went on to even dizzier heights: "There is intelligent life throughout space. To make regular contact we will need solar energy in the coming age of aluminum ... I have discovered the potential of stationary waves in the Earth. By using these waves, we can completely control electrical space, the energy and force for all kinds of power transmission ... I may have already experienced interplanetary communication."

Strange ideas for a man of the nineteenth century? Yes, but Tesla discovered that he could "tune" the frequency of those energy waves, making it possible for them to be "received" at great distances by a system tuned to the same frequency. Marconi, a disciple of Tesla's, took the idea, ran with it, and eventually developed radio transmission. In later years the United States Supreme Court established Tesla's priority as the owner of patents covering radio and other electromagnetic transmissions.

Tesla went to Colorado Springs to build a new laboratory in 1899 because he was sure that just as radio signals are sent and received, electrical power could be distributed to any point on the planet. His experiments soon proved that the Earth was indeed an electrically charged body and that these forces could be manipulated on a global scale.

In one of his many lectures before scientific groups, Tesla revealed his discovery: "The Earth is literally alive with electrical vibrations and soon I was deeply absorbed in this interesting investigation. Impossible as it seemed, *our planet's response to solar vibrations*, despite its vast extent, behaved like a conductor of limited dimensions, making it possible to transmit power in unlimited amounts, to any terrestrial distance and almost without loss."

He had previously produced high-frequency waves through electrical resonance in his wired circuits by "tuning" the electricity. Now he realized that he could reproduce the same effect by using the Earth itself as a huge combination condenser and coil. "By charging it and discharging it rhythmically with high-frequency, high-potential oscillations, the entire Earth can be set in electrical resonance, thus distributing its energy waves to the four corners of the globe."

Resonance though—true resonance—can destroy an object. Alexander, Caesar, and Napoleon, for example, all knew that a division of soldiers marching in unison across a bridge will cause the bridge to crumble. Each object has a special vibratory rate; a glass, for instance, can be shattered when a violin note matches (or resonates with) the vibratory rate of the glass.

Tesla was happy to learn that the Earth has a built-in inhibitor, which made true resonance of the planet impossible. "It is a natural law, Nature's gift to mankind," he said. "Without this planetary resistance to true resonance, the Earth could be destroyed during experiments such as mine. We need to supply the energy lost through the Earth's natural electrical resistance to practical resonance, which will leave us in perfect control of the situation."

The day finally came when Tesla's first transmitting tower at Colorado Springs was ready for the crucial test. He started his generators and set the experiment in motion by pumping electricity into the Earth and drew it out at the rhythmic rate of 150,000 oscillations per second, which produced wavelengths of about 7,000 feet.

John J. O'Neill, then science editor of the New York *Herald Tribune*, reported in his book, *Prodigal Genius*, that "When the moving waves expanded outward from Colorado Springs they travelled in all directions in ever-increasing circles until they passed over the bulge of the Earth, and then in ever-smaller circles and with increasing intensity converged on the diametrically opposite point of the Earth—a trifle to the west of the two French islands, Amsterdam and St. Paul, in the area midway between the southern tip of Africa and the southwest corner of Australia. Here, a tremendous electrical south pole was built up, marked by a wave of great amplitude which rose and fell in unison with Tesla's apparatus at its north pole in Colorado Springs. This sent back an electrical echo from the south antipode to Colorado Springs, producing the same effect, but a mite weaker. Just as it arrived back at Colorado Springs, however, the oscillator was working to build up a wave that would re-enforce it and send it back more powerfully than before. This performance was repeated continuously."

In Tesla's laboratory the coils were tuned in perfect electrical resonance with the surge of energy, which built up potentials of more than *100 million volts!* (Dr. Robert K. Golka's attempt to create fireballs, reported in scientific papers as generating 20 million volts, was described as "the highest voltages ever produced by man.")

It seems astounding now that Tesla used only as much power as you will find under your car's hood—about 300 horsepower—to charge the Earth and produce this tremendous voltage! He demonstrated beyond doubt that a relatively insignificant amount of energy is all that's needed to produce the oscillation. The natural resonating ability of the Earth itself did the rest. It was a simple apparatus, really, using only a version of the same elements as the tuning unit in your radio or TV receiver—hardly anything more than a coil, a condenser with a ground connection, and a twenty-foot antenna. This device, when properly tuned to the same frequency as the Earth's energy waves, can draw that energy off for power, light, heat, and every kind of electrical appliance.

To show that it could be done, Tesla demonstrated his wireless power transmission by brilliantly lighting up 200 incandescent lamps from a distance of twenty-six miles. He developed the idea for a similar energy-distributing system—a lower frequency capable of operating ordinary motors, including automobiles, boats, aircraft—even entire industrial facilities—all of which could draw off the power wirelessly to operate from any place on Earth.

J. P. Morgan and the heads of the great financial institutions of the day were stunned: "Will this new wireless distribution-of-power system fit into the existing economic and financial structure? If it is adopted for development, who would be best suited to control it? Can it be controlled in a practical way when any spot on Earth will be an outlet for an unlimited reservoir of power for anyone who cares enough to tap it with a simple device?

"It boils down to three choices," Morgan said to several colleagues when they first learned of Tesla's success. "It's either Edison's system, which is distributing energy over wires for about one hundred miles, Tesla's alternating current system, which is certainly far more efficient—or this new wireless system."

Naturally it was no contest. How could they collect compensation for services rendered? Tesla had developed a worldwide wireless superpower system with one terrible flaw: *it was free*, and therefore it was virtually impossible to gain a monopoly over it. After Tesla constructed an even greater transmitting tower at Wardenclyffe, on Long Island, the work slowed down, almost strangled in red tape—even sabotaged. Then Morgan withdrew all his money and stopped Tesla's work dead in its tracks.

All of the inventor's notes are not in the museum in Belgrade. On January 8, 1943, when his body was found the day after his death, a group of FBI agents confiscated all his personal notes and papers and immediately locked them up somewhere in the archives of the government. We *were* at war then, after all, so quite naturally the great transmitting tower had to be destroyed. *Everything* had to be destroyed or buried in secret vaults of the federal archives. Just imagine the terrible things that might have happened if the United States and the U. S. S. R., in an hour of sublime sanity, had decided to exchange all Tesla's surviving work and cooperate in developing it for the advancement of the human species, as Tesla had often requested? Think of how far the world might have advanced if such a miracle had happened.

Once, while discussing the growing schism between his religious parents' beliefs (his father was a Serbian Orthodox priest) and his own humanitarian scientific urges, young Tesla tried to explain: "You say *you* love people. I don't. It is mankind that I love."

CHAPTER 7

Velikovsky: Destroyer of Worlds

Every age produces its share of geniuses. Occasionally a rare figure emerges with an extraordinary idea or a theory powerful enough to change some avenue of history. Whether or not we accept Freud's sex and dream interpretations, he was one of these people. So was Chaim Weizmann, the Father of Zionism. So also was Albert Einstein, whose Theory of Relativity revolutionized our ideas of time and space.

Each of these men faced varying forms of opposition. In addition to numerous less obvious characteristics, they had two interesting things in common: all were Jews, and—at one time or another—all were friends of Immanuel Velikovsky, easily recognized as today's most controversial figure in the world of science—or science fiction, depending on your bias.

Until Velikovsky's enormously popular book, *Worlds in Collision*, was published in 1950, most orthodox natural scientists simply accepted that the Earth, its oceans, ice caps, rivers, forests, deserts, mountains, and plains evolved peacefully—*gradually*—during millions, if not billions, of years.

"Super-scholar" Velikovsky threw down the gauntlet before geologists, anthropologists, paleontologists, and practically every other "ologist" in the early 1950s. He suggested global *catastrophism*, i.e., the idea that evolution takes place under conditions of almost unimaginable violence.

Orthodoxy scoffed when Velikovsky suggested that the fabled lost world of Atlantis might actually have existed and might have been destroyed during a great cataclysm, just as Plato described. Since then, the combined efforts of Athens University and America's Woods Hole Oceanographic Institution have revealed that a terrible convulsion of the Earth actually did coincide with a volcanic eruption exceeding that of Krakatoa itself (the worst volcanic explosion in remembered history) and that the ancient blast covered thousands of square miles and completely obliterated a whole culture—an entire civilization, the story of which has come down the ages to us as the legend of Atlantis.

Velikovsky was and is reviled by most scientists for claiming that the great mountain chains of the world were cast aloft during the time of historical man—and that living, intelligent human beings witnessed and recorded these titanic events less than 4,000 years ago!

He insisted that a comet, the present planet Venus, "attacked" the Earth mere centuries after being ejected from Jupiter, the largest planet in our solar system, and that it did so—from the geologic and astronomic viewpoint—quite recently.

Is Velikovsky right after all? His erudition and his mastery of several disciplines—not to mention the remarkable accuracy of his predictions—are now convincing growing numbers of space-age scientists and technicians who refuse to go along with "old-guard" astronomers, geologists, and paleontologists in their support of Lyall's idea of "slow evolutionary processes." The furor Velikovsky created in scientific circles is actually increasing rather than quietly dying a "natural" death.

This controversy—Cataclysm versus Uniformism—reverberates anew each time an American or Russian space probe to Venus, Jupiter, Mars, or the Moon confirms Velikovsky's prescience about the real facts of the solar system: (1) that Mars is cratered like our Moon; (2) that Venus is extremely hot; (3) that raw petroleum deep within the Earth is not billions or even millions but mere *thousands* of years old!

When Sigmund Freud published "Moses and Monotheism" in the late 1930s, Velikovsky, who knew him, was inspired to write a critical essay entitled "Freud and His Heroes" (Oedipus, Akhnaton, and Moses). It was published in the October, 1941, issue of *The Psychoanalytic Review* as "The Dreams Freud Dreamed." Several apparent historical anomalies struck him (on the basis of the evidence) as inevitably the result of a universal catastrophe—a disaster of global dimensions and consequences.

Velikovsky seems almost destined to have arrived at a rebuttal of Lyall's idea of "Gradualism." During his remarkable life, he discovered an overwhelming number of paradoxes. One of these was that, according to Lyall and Darwin's evolutionary ideas, the body and mind of man, admittedly an enormously sophisticated biological apparatus spanning at least 10 million years of evolution, were able to produce a recorded history of only a few *thousand* years!

From the time he was born on June 10, 1895, in Vitebsk, Russia, the youngest of three sons, Velikovsky was subtly, inexorably led toward a revolutionary understanding of cosmology. His father combined Hebrew scholarship with his business. Before Immanuel was ten, his mother had taught him to speak several languages. He distinguished himself in Russian and mathematics at the Medvednikov Gymnasium before graduating with a gold medal.

He then left Russia and studied medicine at Montpelier in southern France. Smarting because, as a Jew, he was unable to enter a Russian university, he organized and became the leader of a group of expatriate Russian Jewish students, many of whom were ardent Zionists. Velikovsky fell under the spell of Zionism and gave up his studies to visit and then study in Palestine. Unsatisfied, he enrolled during the following term at the University of Edinburgh and took premedical courses in zoology, botany, and biology.

When the First World War broke out, Velikovsky found himself trapped in Russia while visiting his home on a summer vacation. He registered at the "Free University" in Moscow—an institution formed by the dean and professors of the Moscow Imperial

University who had resigned en masse to protest interference with their academic freedom. There, Velikovsky studied history, law, and economics, and by 1915 was able to resume his medical education at the University of Moscow, where he received his degree in 1921—just about the time his parents emigrated to Palestine.

With the burning idea of establishing a Jewish university in Berlin, Velikovsky co-authored the *Scripta Universitatis* with the famed German scholar Dr. Heinrich Loewe. It was a series of volumes with articles by the world's best Jewish thinkers. Albert Einstein edited the mathematics and physics volumes. Chaim Weizmann, the famed scientist and leader of the World Zionist Organization (who was to become Israel's first president), offered his support and asked Velikovsky to start a Hebrew University in Palestine.

Instead, Velikovsky married Elisheva Kramer and went to work as a general practitioner in Palestine and Jerusalem from 1924 until 1939. As a result of his exposure to Freud, he wanted further experience in psychoanalysis, and he therefore studied in Vienna under Dr. Wilhelm Stekel. Velikovsky practiced as an analyst in Haifa and Tel Aviv, and published numerous psychological papers, several of them in Freud's *Imago*. Velikovsky was among the first to suggest that epileptic characteristics could be diagnosed medically by encephalograms.

He began a new and ambitious series called *Scripta Academica Hierosolymitana*, to which Chaim Weizmann submitted the first paper in biochemistry.

In order to do research for "Freud and His Heroes," Velikovsky brought his family to New York in the summer of 1939, fully expecting to stay only eight months. During his visit, however, he discovered proof that the historical prototype of Oedipus actually was Akhnaton. (The result of this research was published as a book by Doubleday in 1960 under the title *Oedipus and Akhnaton*.) His researches kept Velikovsky in America far longer than the expected eight months; the deeper he probed, the more convinced he became that some "great universal catastrophe" had occurred during comparatively recent historical times—incredibly enough, within the memory of historical man. His investigation became feverish, almost obsessive, and he never returned to Palestine. The entire course of his life was radically changed.

Velikovsky grew almost psychically obsessed about the origin of the Dead Sea. "Was it," he wondered, "formed in the days of the Exodus, when Mount Sinai erupted, and some debacle took place at the Sea of Passage?" Was the catastrophe *also* experienced in Egypt? "Does an Egyptian document speak of a similar catastrophe?" The key proved to be a papyrus carrying the lamentations of an Egyptian scholar named Ipuwer. Velikovsky consulted famous Egyptologists and discovered that the papyrus not only contained a description of a natural catastrophe but also of the plagues, exactly as the Bible related them (for further discussion, see the final chapters).

Amazingly, he found other parallels in history and a chronology in the legends and myths of the Amerindians, the Hindus, the Huns, Slavs, Polynesians—in fact, all the peoples of the ancient world. His conclusion was that science's understanding of the chronology of ancient times was totally wrong. He reconstructed the history of Egypt and the Near East from the end of the Middle Kingdom to the death of Alexander the Great in 322 B.C.

Velikovsky instantly dropped his work on "Freud and His Heroes" and began writing a new book, *Ages in Chaos*. But even while working on *this* book, he began to wonder about the exact *nature* of the catastrophe that destroyed the whole Middle Kingdom of Egypt. The Book of Joshua described colossal meteors roaring out of the skies—huge showers of stones, *and the appearance of the Sun standing motionless in the heavens!* Could these phenomena have been caused by some anomalous, ubiquitous *cosmic* event?

Almost frantically, Velikovsky began studying Mexican and Chinese sources. Everywhere he searched, there were references to Venus and/or a huge cometary body that rivaled the Sun in brilliance! (It is an astronomical fact that some comets exceed Jupiter's size—and even surpass the Sun in volume.) To Velikovsky, it seemed self-evident that Venus was connected to—if not the cause of—the upheavals on Earth.

Once again, the course of his researches became dual, and he devoted nearly all his time to writing *Ages in Chaos* and *Worlds in Collision*.

The controversy still rages, even though colleges across the nation—Princeton, Dartmouth, the University of Chicago, the University of Kansas, the University of St. Louis, the University of Wisconsin and numerous others, including the staid Rittenhouse Astronomical Society of Philadelphia—are now begging for all the Velikovsky they can get.

The breadth and influence of Velikovsky's work was almost overwhelming. I wanted a closer, more intimate view of the scientist who, in 1967, seemed to have had more impact on historians' outlook than any living man. (You can learn how Velikovsky's attackers and critics have been rebutted, point by point, by reading physicist C. J. Ransom, Ph.D. His 274-page book, *The Age of Velikovsky*, reveals the irrationality of many of the so-called scientific rebuttals to Velikovsky. Dr. Ransom may be reached through LAR Research, 5413 Stephanie Drive, Fort Worth, Texas 76117.)

When I showed up for the appointment to interview Dr. Velikovsky, my wife, Evelyn, and two children were with me. His wife, Elisheva, entertained Evelyn, my then three-year-old son Danny, and five-year-old daughter Maria on the porch and in the garden. She served them bowls of freshly sliced cold fruit.

After the long summer afternoon of intensive interviewing I was surprised to see the man who had single-handedly revolutionized the entire foundation of the scientific and historical world thoroughly enjoying the kids. Before we left, he autographed a copy of *Worlds in Collision* for my wife, with the notation "You have most charming children."

I had originally envisioned Velikovsky as a kind of Don Quixote, but nevertheless admired his spirit for upsetting the stuffed shirts of sciencedom. His own "dragons"—abuse, disrespect, and published attacks against him as a "crackpot"—have not diminished with time. In some cases, the attacks have intensified.

Meanwhile, despite the strongest efforts of the Committee for the Scientific Investigation of Claims of the Paranormal, Velikovskiism has become almost standard fare with a new generation that has grown up with greater familiarity with ancient catastrophism. Thousands of future scientists have been influenced by *Worlds in Collision*, *Earth in Upheaval*, *Ages in Chaos*, *Oedipus and Akhnaton*, and *Peoples of the Sea*. The text of my interview with Velikovsky follows.

Question: In *Worlds in Collision*, you said that some comets visit the solar system at a rate of about one every two years—500 in a century—and have "an average period of about 10,000 years." Taking that *average*, how could anyone be really certain about a comet that had, say, a period of 30,000 years?

Velikovsky: Comets of long duration visit the solar system at a rate of 500 a century. That's about five a year. In the solar system we know the comets but not their *exact* periods because they are disturbed in their motion by the larger planets.* The "comet" that has the shortest period—Venus, for example, has 224.7 days—that is, the solar year of Venus. Mercury is 88 days. The comet that has the shortest period of duration is 3.4 years, I believe. This is an Enke-comet. . . .

Question: Which comet is that?

Velikovsky: Enke. E-N-K-E. Every 3.4 years, she makes one revolution. The Earth orbits the

---

*And at their close approach to an apparent dark body that seems to have made ours a binary star system.

Sun in one year, Venus, 224 days, Mercury 88 days. Enke comet is the shortest of the short-period comets. There are so many of those comets that they repeatedly return to the solar system; we know when they will return. Halley's comet is one of them; it is supposed to be the farthest, but there may be one even farther out. Halley's comet has a period between 74 and 76 years, depending on how disturbed its orbit is. Between the longest- and the shortest-period comets, there are many more which are divided into groups; those that reach within the orbit of Jupiter are called the Jovian family. Within the orbit of Saturn, they are called the Saturnian family. The largest group is the Jovian family. There are groups that reach Neptune; among them is Halley's comet. The solar orbit of Jupiter is twelve years and Saturn is thirty years. And so it goes . . . after Saturn—no comets at all. No comets between 100 to 500 years. . . .

Question: What about the orbit of Pluto?

Velikovsky: One second. There are *no* comets that have a 500-year period. There is an interval after this seventy-six-year period during which comets are *supposed* to return. No one knows if they will *ever* return. Whether they do or not depends on when you observe them, whether they move in an elliptical orbit—a closed orbit, or a parabolic orbit, which is to say, infinity—unclosed. The parabolic orbit reaches the Sun, swings around and goes the other way. Some of them are parabolic. If they are not disturbed, you have to accept the view that they do not belong to the solar system—that they will *never* return again. One theory is that there is a family of billions of comets on the periphery of the solar system; this to say—a *sphere* of comets. From here and there, they change. It is believed that they are deflected by an unseen body or by forces from neighboring stars. From such influence they may lose their way, come out of the "sphere" and approach the Sun as long-period comets.

Question: I've never heard that solarian comets could be influenced by other stars.

Velikovsky: This is the view of a Dutch astronomer named Oort and is accepted by orthodox scientists, who believe Oort has provided the best explanation. Dr. Whipple, director of the Smithsonian Institution at Harvard, came up with the question, "Why is this period of comets necessary?" Neptune was discovered in 1846, about sixty or seventy years after the discovery of Uranus. Neptune was discovered by two men who observed planetary irregularities. *Something* was disturbing Uranus in its orbit, and they wanted to discover what the disturbing force was. They hypothesized that it was another planet, and from this were able to roughly calculate its position. But this did not explain *what* the disturbing force was. They searched for something unknown, and eventually one more planet was found—Pluto. But Pluto was so small it could not *possibly* have disturbed the larger inner planets. You could not see Pluto through a telescope as a disc—as you can with the other planets, you see. . . .

Question: What we're trying to learn is how does this relate, specifically, to the idea that comets, whose orbital periods *average* 10,000 years, were remembered—*ever*—by anyone on Earth?

Velikovsky: It could not. Only by the fact that such comets do exist.

Question: Good enough. You cite many instances of cometary periods being deflected and retarded by planets such as Jupiter, Saturn, and even the Earth. If the comet Venus orbited the solar system, as you claim your evidence shows, would it not have been deflected by near-passages with Jupiter or Saturn? And, conversely, wouldn't it have been too massive to be a true comet?

Velikovsky: There's no question that in modern times no comets of this size were observed. But as Professor Bobronikov, Director of Perkins Observatory, wrote in 1951 in a book, *Astrophysics*—

Question: Where is Perkins Observatory?

Velikovsky: In Ohio. Bobronikov stated that several comets that were seen during the last century were extraordinarily large—the size and mass, say, of the Moon. The opposition to the view that no comet could be as large as a planet is, consequently, undermined. It couldn't be too far-fetched because the Moon is only one order of magnitude smaller than Mercury. Now along comes Whipple who claims that Pluto was originally a comet. Pluto is not large, as planets go, but nevertheless it *is* a planet! Whipple claims that Pluto was originally a comet because it moves along an elliptical orbit, because it does not move in the ecliptic, but on an angle of 17 degrees from the ecliptic—and because he needs this for his explanation of that *sphere* of comets that swing, so to say, all around the periphery of the solar system, which I previously mentioned. This body of comets is sometimes disturbed by neighboring stars. Both Whipple and Oort subscribe to this theory . . . that one of those comets settled in the solar system as Pluto. Now, if you permit this for Pluto, you must also permit it for Venus. You cannot make a selection between male and female.

Question: Still, to use the existence and/or acceptance of Pluto as a comet—or a possible proto-comet—and say, well, "Venus was a comet which is the same as the idea that Pluto was a comet," is a weak argument. Nevertheless, your evidence does seem to be stronger in reference to Venus than Whipple's in reference to Pluto. Dr. Whipple is now hypothesizing a sort of "cosmic snowstorm" which originated from Jupiter and formed the outer planets.

Velikovsky: This is very interesting—something I did not know.

Question: Some physicists still claim that in order for your theories to work, you ignore the laws of gravity and the laws of motion. In view of the fact that Albert Einstein himself supported your views, how would you answer these charges?

Velikovsky: In the first place, I would say that Einstein didn't really support my views; he was interested in my work and discussed it with me, especially during the last years of his life and more so in the last few *months* of his life. Once, we had had two long sessions—until midnight—in March and again in April before he died. He was definitely interested because he was giving in. Nevertheless, he was visibly shaken, because in our conversations and debates, especially around June, 1954, I wrote him a letter which asked the same, ever-recurring question: "Aside from gravitation and inertia, were there other forces participating in the celestial mechanism?" *I claimed that electricity and magnetism are NOT absent. Whatever role these forces played, they WERE present.* This was not acceptable to scientists, and he put this to me in writing. But in that letter in June, I offered to solve the problem. I wrote, "Jupiter sends out radio noises. Let us put our discussion to a crucial test. If you wish, this could be easily done." I have my original letter with his marginal notes, but he didn't do anything in that respect. And then in April of 1955 there was an announcement by Dr. Franklin and Dr. Burker of the Carnegie Institution in Washington that radio noises were coming from Jupiter. In the same year (1955), they discovered and announced it ten months after my letter to Einstein. They were perplexed; actually for weeks they didn't know what it was that they had discovered. They looked for radio disturbances in the neighborhood, and the noises were finally deduced to emanate from an extraterrestrial source because the Earth takes 365 days to make one orbit of the Sun, but 366 days in relation to the fixed stars. The Sun rises two minutes earlier each day toward the vernal equinox and sets two minutes later. This four-minute differential adds up to slightly more than a twenty-four-hour day in the course of a year. What I wish to say is that I related this information to Einstein from the story as it broke in *The New York Times,* and he was very much taken by it. This was nine days before his death; in fact, it was his last conversation with me about the subject.

Now I'd like to finish answering your *previous* question. *The noninclusion of electricity and magnetism in the celestial mechanism is completely REVERSED now!* Today, all scientists agree—and every astronomer *knows*—that the Sun ejects great "tongues" of plasma, that interplanetary space is magnetic, that the Earth has a magnetosphere, that Jupiter has a *very* strong magnetosphere, emits radio noises, and so on. So you cannot deny that the satellites of Jupiter, some of them very close to the primary, are not influenced by Jupiter. The next one, Io, is the same distance as the Moon is from the Earth. How could they *possibly* move through the magnetosphere of Jupiter without being influenced? Or, for that matter, how could Jupiter itself move through the interplanetary magnetic field without being influenced. So-o-o-o, these views today are no longer heretical as they once were. They are accepted. Actually, if you go to the library today and take down a book on astronomy written in 1950 by Dr. Whipple, it is as though you are reading something by Regiomontanus in the sixteenth century. This is because our knowledge has increased to the point where many of the beliefs once held are no longer true. Just read a book on astronomy written only fifty years ago and you'll find the subject is entirely different than it is today. Today it's all about plasma; it's about magnetic fields, it's about alpha particles, it's about the magnetosphere. There's very little of the old beliefs we once accepted as the final word. All of a sudden, astronomers became electron astronomers, radio astronomers, astrophysicists. Previously the most sophisticated form of optical astronomy was spectroscopy. Today there is radio telescopy; you actually *hear* the stars instead of seeing them! The question now is no longer a problem of whether I am wrong or right; it is all there in my books and in recent discovery. The question now is *"How strong is participation in the interplanetary electromagnetic force fields?"*

Question: In three of your books, *Worlds in Collision*, *Earth in Upheaval*, and *Ages in Chaos*, you continually refer to the coincidence of various disastrous phenomena occurring at once—stones falling from the sky, the eruption of thousands of volcanoes at once, the rains of fire, naptha, and hydrocarbons (actually raw petroleum), the devastating typhoons, earthquakes, oceanic flooding of continents, the actual stopping of the Earth's rotation for a period of at least a week. Entire species of animals became extinct at once. Yet despite enormous numbers of casualties, the human race managed to survive. We find the fossilized bones of millions of animals all over the world—some with flesh and skin still attached—but little or no evidence of the *human* casualties of the global disasters. Why is this?

Velikovsky: It is *not* so. You can find plenty of them. Wherever you look—every place on Earth, you will find them, both artifacts *and* human bones. Only recently I received a clipping from somebody about the finding of bones of human beings among those of extinct animals. This is my whole stance in *Earth in Upheaval*—the artifacts of prehistoric man in the wreckage of an entire paleontological age. There are many early human artifacts in Melbourne, Australia, and Indian River in Florida. And in many, many other places you will find instances of humans perishing en masse with the animals. Some animals perished completely—they became extinct. Other animals perished on this continent but *not* on another—camels and horses in America, for example. The fact that we have horses thriving in America today is because they were *re*introduced here by the conquering Spaniards. So it was with human beings. In many places on the various continents, man was destroyed to the last—Atlantis—or the entire civilization of Minoa, perhaps. But not *all* people. In answer to what you asked with regard to the Earth's stopping for a period of a week or two, it is not proper to state it quite that way. The Earth was disturbed in its rotation, and its revolution; its axis was continually changing its direction. In that sense, it was not actually standing still. It was disturbed. It could not proceed properly. So when it resumed its rotation, it was in a different orbit, it had a different speed of rotation, so it was a different year, a different month, a different number of days in the month. But it did not stand still, like—like the wife of Lot.

Question: Your amazingly accurate predictions based upon the picture of global devastation you have presented from apparent facts can't be ignored. Had there been a questioning or general scientific inquiry into *how* you were able to predict the temperature of Venus, the craters of Mars, and the retrograde axial spin of Venus?

Velikovsky: The type of inquiry you have in mind was not organized or undertaken. There were some efforts made in that direction, like Professor Hess, Chairman of Space, Board of the National Academy of Sciences, and who is with NASA. He convened the first open meeting of the Cosmos and Chronos group to discuss my work, my thesis, and the reception by scientists to my books. We held open meetings here on the Princeton University campus. Such Cosmos and Chronos groups have also been organized on other campuses. There was an effort made by the chancellor of the University of California at Los Angeles, Dr. Franklin Murphy, in January, 1964. And he turned to the then chairman of the geophysics department, Professor Slichter, with a request to organize a commission from various departments to investigate that which was proven *true* in my work and why my books were greeted by such an emotional outburst. Professor Slichter refused to undertake this assignment, and the reason for his refusal was not made clear to me. However, by the end of that year, I found out. My correspondent at the university, Chancellor Murphy, wrote that Professor Slichter had obtained some other assignment upon his retirement —for the government. To which I answered, "But, Dr. Murphy, you did not undertake this study to supply Dr. Slichter with work, but to try to learn why a theory so much in harmony with newly discovered facts and in such discord with accepted views is not accepted. It is incumbent upon you to try to learn which view is correct and which is wrong." Well, I received no satisfactory answer to this, and the entire question was put to rest until the end of that year when I discovered that Dr. Slichter had refused the assignment in January, 1964, in response to Chancellor Murphy's request b-e-c-a-u-s-e . . . as he said, "A man like Velikovsky who claims that the magnetosphere can reach such a distance as the Moon *doesn't know what he is talking about*! He has no understanding of scientific matters whatever. His views are far removed from possibility." In that same year, 1964, in the Los Angeles *Times*, Dr. Ness's discovery that the magnetosphere reaches the Moon was published. This was subsequently brought to the attention of Dr. Slichter, who expressed great amazement, especially because Dr. Ness was my own former collaborator. He abrogated his assignment and never attempted to pursue the question further.

Question: After carefully reading *Worlds in Collision*, and noting that the historical records of practically all ancient peoples spoke of the destruction and separation of many World Ages through fire, earthquake, hurricane, and flood, you get the impression that it can happen again. *Will* it occur once more?

Velikovsky: There is no doubt that the peril we face from the recurrence of such global disasters is indeed great. However, I personally believe that the peril we face from the hand of man himself is much greater. Because man has the ability now to destroy himself and the Earth as well. But as to the chance that the Earth will have a collision with some planetary bodies, it seems at the moment to be unlikely. Each planet in its orbit remains separate from all others. There are no interchangeable orbits except those of Pluto and Neptune, and they are not in the same plane, so it would take a long time for something like this to happen. And besides, you know, since the discovery of Neptune in 1846, only 121 years ago, the orbit of that planet is more than *double* that period! So we have not yet observed Neptune even in half of its orbit. Pluto was discovered in 1930, so we have seen only one tenth or an eighth of its orbit. At certain times, Pluto is farther from the Earth than Neptune. Tomorrow, perhaps, Pluto is closer to the Earth than Neptune. So they are interchangeable in their orbits; it just happened recently. Now they are on different planes. So the planets are not now in a position to collide, except some satellites, such as the satellites of Jupiter, which do make up combatical figures, but do not collide. The first asteroid was discovered in the first night of the nineteenth century. Since then, many more have been discovered. At first they were found only between Mars and Jupiter. Then some of them were placed across the orbit of Mars, then there were some found to be crossing the orbit of the Earth itself. One of these was Hermes, which passed us in 1937—only 350,000 miles from us.*

Question: The largest of these is Ceres, is it not?

Velikovsky: Ceres. I believe you are right. I think Ceres was the first to be discovered. However, a scientist I know announced his computation recently that if the asteroid Icarus, on returning from the Sun, will be disturbed by Mercury at a certain angle, it *could* collide with the Earth. So you could very well have a kind of a panic.

Question: You say the present orbit of the solar system is so stable that nothing like the previous global catastrophes can occur again. And yet, was not the solar system so stable 4,000 years ago that *nothing* like a systemwide upset could possibly have been foreseen?

Velikovsky: About 3,500 years ago, the protoplanet Venus came very close to the Earth. But this didn't happen *immediately* after Venus escaped from Jupiter. It had been orbiting the Sun for hundreds of thousands—if not millions—of years before. The birth of Venus was a result of Jupiter and Saturn disturbing each other.

Question: The intellectual as well as emotional impact of your work seems to have changed the thinking of an entire generation. If we're around long enough, it may influence the philosophy of generations yet to come. Assuming that another catastrophe will overtake us, what are we capable of doing to assure that our knowledge, at least, will be transferred into the next world age?

Velikovsky: Well, this is the first time that I've

---

* Since this interview, the rings of Uranus and a new "planet" (called Object Kowal now orbiting between Jupiter and Saturn) have been discovered.

ever heard this question. The records of man could be preserved in the safest places, this would be the caves, which are actually not always safe; they may collapse during a universal disaster and be shut up for eons, which may actually be the case now. We could put satellites in orbit. Or we could build shelters for the purpose of preserving the best our world had produced, such as the Pharaohs did in the time of ancient Egyptian catastrophes.

Question: The time capsules of the day?

Velikovsky: Well, in the years following the use of the atomic bombs, when the fear of nuclear holocaust was universal, I recall having received some letters, notably one from a postal clerk in Philadelphia, urging me to preserve my books and manuscripts on microfilm somewhere in the Earth inside a time capsule.

Question: In your estimation, what is the possibility that a new cosmic upheaval will destroy all life on Earth—or even the Earth itself?

Velikovsky: I believe you touched on this earlier, and I said there is a far greater chance that man will be the instrument of his own destruction because man is a victim of amnesia. The fact that this catastrophe took place so recently, in a historical sense—and despite the fact that we have overwhelming evidence among paleontological, archaeological, and geological records but also in literary records themselves—that terrible catastrophes have occurred to this planet—that the greatest mathematical and astronomical observations and texts completely agree with the stories describing the experiences of eyewitnesses (*or whether you wish to call it mythology*) that life on the planet Earth was decimated in the time of historical man. Actually, you don't have to dig very deeply to look for it; it's all there, around us—again and again and again. Nevertheless, we read it and do not recognize the significance of what we are reading. By far, the vast majority of ancient texts deal specifically with the phenomenon of catastrophism. In the Old Testament we read of geological disturbances in which a mountain melts like wax, the sea being torn apart or erupting on the land, and cosmic debris bombarding the people, and the oceans parting to show the foundations of the Earth—and *we* say all these things are simply metaphors! This is our inability to see, our inability to remember what actually occurred—and this is what makes it appear to me that mankind is a victim of collective amnesia. As such a victim, he likes to play with atomic weapons; it looks as though he actively seeks, with thermonuclear weapons, to *repeat* the events that took place! The victim of amnesia who has undergone a traumatic experience seems to want to relive those experiences again.

Question: You speak of collective amnesia and also of world devastation. Is it, in your estimation, possible—considering the discrepancy between man's true antiquity and the shortness of his recorded history—that humanity might have achieved a state of technological and scientific civilization comparable with our *present* age—sometime before in history?

Velikovsky: There *were* civilizations like ours that were destroyed! There's no question *whatever* of this. We see the so-called Old Bronze Civilization of ancient Egypt was destroyed in universal catastrophes, the Middle Kingdoms were destroyed in catastrophes. Civilization at that time had risen to great heights, where events similar to those of today had *previously* occurred. These civilizations are now buried so deeply within the lower strata of the Earth that we simply do not have archaeological evidence of their existence. But we have *abundant* references in literature—even in rabbinical literature—that many times before, and I quote, that *before* this present Earth Age existed (in fact *several times*), the *same* Earth was created—then it was leveled and *re*-created; all civilizations were buried. This was long, long *before* the time of the biblical character Adam.

Question: You speak almost as though you were an orthodox Jew. Do you believe in, or accept a theological or purposeful explanation for creation—that is, for the existence of everything?

Velikovsky: No, no, not at all. This is one of those things that in several places in my books I reveal my own conviction on this subject. People are grasping for something; they look for it in my writings and they cannot find it. They write to me very often on this question. I believe I answered only once when a group from a prison in Illinois wrote to me that this occupies their minds very much and they debated and would like to know how I stand. To men in such a distressful situation, I felt that I owed an answer and I wrote to them. But generally, I keep such things to myself because it's just the same as asking whether William Conrad Roentgen, who discovered X-rays, believed that X-rays were created by God or not. The problem is not whether he was a churchgoer or an atheist; this is not the question at all. The *fact* is that he discovered X-rays. Now you can approach it from the philosophical viewpoint and say, "This is the creation of the Lord," and you would be perfectly right. If you are a disbeliever and claim that X-rays are the result of a soulless Nature, you are consequentially correct. But you should not confuse historical or scientific questions with theological considerations.

Question: You seem to suggest that the entire planetary system becomes unbalanced at somewhat regular intervals, causing the flip of the Earth on its axis, the super-perigee movement of Mars, and/or the creation of a new planet such as Venus, from the gas giants beyond Mars. Do you think this is an important enough factor for astronauts to be concerned with in the exploration of other worlds?

Velikovsky: No. You did not exactly present my views correctly, and I would not blame you, because the publisher put these claims on the jacket—that suddenly the planets run amok. The fact is, they *didn't* run amok. Various worlds interchanged orbits. There were disturbances between them; there were other disturbances caused by the planetary bodies coming into close contact, as well as by the gravitational pull and electromagnetic exchanges among the planets. There were also electrical discharges, so you can expect there were additional effects, but nothing *beyond* scientific reason or *against* the laws of Nature. Everything occurred *within* the laws of Nature as we understand them, and the laws of celestial mechanics were *never* upset! The mechanism was disturbed, but not the mechanics.

Question: If our own solar system becomes an agent of human and animal destruction every few thousand years, do you think this also occurs in *other* planetary systems? If so, is there any synchronism between our disasters and those, say, of Alpha Centauri, Tau Ceti, or Epsilon Erdani?

Velikovsky: I don't really know what is going on in other solar systems. I can only say what I found in the records of *this* solar system. If this solar system presents any basis for making deductions about other remote or alien systems, then perhaps they too undergo such disturbances, with equal results to the inhabitants of other worlds. Not so long ago, astronomers believed that it was only by the most remote chance that another star could support another planetary system. Today the scientific view has changed; it is now believed that most, if not all, stars support planetary systems. Right now, I wouldn't take any stand about this because as you can see in my works, I didn't make any hypothesis concerning the future or about other star systems. I tried to explore the

Earthly past and explain it in understandable terms. What I found in history, myth, and legend, I tried to find correlations in such phenomena as astronomy, celestial mechanics, geology, anthropology, archaeology, paleontology, and all these sciences in order to find interdisciplinary evidence of all the pertinent factors. But I did not, in any place, avow an hypothesis unless I *indicated* that something could be so. In that case, I clearly stated my conviction. Otherwise, I claimed that I had *no* hypothesis or theory to explain anything. What I tried to do, in the main, was to reconcile the past.

Question: You stated that Mars can be said to have saved the Earth from a major catastrophe by colliding with Venus, that Venus was dreaded by Earthmen for about 700 years. As long as much of your evidence comes from historical records, legends, and myths, why is it that ancient astrologers viewed Mars as evil and Venus as good?

Velikovsky: I really wasn't aware that Venus was considered beneficial and Mars as adverse. But as you know, I cannot be counted among the astrologers or the supporters of astrology, therefore I am not obliged to provide you with facts. However, let me say that I don't know exactly how the modern astronomers feel, but in the past you will find that the attitude toward Venus among the astrologers during ancient times was that its influence was evil. And it was called Lucifer. Why Lucifer? Because the translation of Lucifer was "carrying light." A carrier of light shouldn't have been regarded as a devil. Both the morning star and evening star is a beautiful sight. Why should it have been regarded as a devil? Another name for Venus was Beelzebub. Nevertheless, you again find the same Venus in the memories and writings of ancient peoples. Don't forget they had the same ideas, the same experience, the metaphors—the symbolism of Venus which came from many quarters: whole populations changed places, they were decimated here, destroyed there, migrated en masse from other places during the same universal catastrophe. And so, in Greek mythology you find the same ideas and legends—that is, the same visual images and mental pictures as are found historically among other races of people. They migrated together. They described the same phenomena, their peculiar viewpoint. They could see Jupiter and Saturn as husband and wife, or father and son—or anything of today when America alone has enough bombs to pulverize everything on the face of the Earth several times over, and so do an increasing number of nations—and if some insane finger pushes the button . . .

Question: Then would you, as a doctor and a psychiatrist, say that we are faced with a form of mass human insanity?

Velikovsky (thoughtfully, quietly): I would say rather that it is a mass amnesia. (A long pause; he speaks slowly.) Mass amnesia is a very dangerous situation indeed.

CHAPTER 8
Scientists in Collusion

"It's part of my business to separate the crackpots from the geniuses," said John W. Campbell, the hard-hitting, trail-blazing editor of *Analog*, the most successful and innovative of all science fiction (and fact) publications. He added, "It's my considered opinion that the author of *Worlds in Collision* is just that—a crackpot."

This was in 1960, ten years after Immanuel Velikovsky had set the scientific world on its ear with his best-selling book challenging the most basic concepts of modern science. Its main theme was that a global cataclysm had overthrown all nations in the time of Moses and separated two distinct World Ages.

Campbell's reaction posed an interesting paradox: something of a Socratic gadfly, he always took pride in the fact that he had liberally showcased many scientifically bizarre and unorthodox views in his magazine. He once presented convincing evidence that the positions of the planets "damned well do influence the weather, and indirectly all living things—including humans." This opened him to accusations of being pro-astrology—a "no-no" among his quarter-million scientifically trained and technically oriented readers.

Velikovsky knew about this, and during one of several interviews I had with him, gave me the distinct impression that he thought *astrologers* were a bunch of crackpots. He didn't want anybody connecting his theories to any astrological beliefs. "There's enough unorthodoxy in my work," he observed wryly, "enough and to spare."

There are scientists, engineers, doctors, and psychiatrists who also happen to be astrologers. I know three astrologers (all NASA scientists, by the way) who think Velikovsky is nuttier than a fruitcake. Then there are Velikovskiian catastrophists who are also astrologers, scientists who think astrologers are all dingbats but who support Velikovsky's views, and—well, however many combinations there are, probably.

Velikovsky disputed both evolution and astronomy by claiming that Venus was a comet only 3,500 years ago, that it had been ejected from the giant planet Jupiter to spin like a billiard ball through the solar system before assuming its present peaceful retrograde orbit. He said that Mars had left its orbit and had headed toward the Earth until a near-collision was intercepted by the Moon's gravitational field. The evidence he gave to support such a bizarre theme was a scholarly, well-written interpretation of the sacred writings of many ancient cultures plus the geological proof "found in the stones and fossilized bones" buried deep in the Earth.

To their everlasting shame, the professional scientists ganged up and forced his publisher, Macmillan, to dump Velikovsky's books by organizing what amounted to a strike against the textbook division. Macmillan capitulated by transferring the scholar's contract to Doubleday, which had no textbook division.

But instead of disappearing, as every hoax should, Velikovsky's theories continued to attract highly skilled and intelligent believers. The peak of his quarter-century crusade was reached in February, 1974, when the American Association for the Advancement of Science invited him to be their featured speaker, after twenty-five years of shabby treatment and personal abuse.

Then seventy-seven years old, the tall, battle-weary heretic, white-maned and imposing as an Old Testament patriarch, strode to the speaker's podium and received a standing ovation from a younger and more conciliatory audience. However, the American Association for the Advancement of Science's gesture was just a brief respite from the continuing storm of controversy, which flared anew.

Sciencedom was automatically and uniformly anti-Velikovsky. But the pro-Velikovsky camp more than made up for their lack of numbers by sheer exuberance and relentless loyalty. And American and Soviet space exploration strengthened his case. Every time one of his uncanny predictions was vindicated by a lunar probe, a Venus fly-by, or a Mars landing, the ranks of his supporters swelled.

Despite this, his harshest critics became even more virulent. In an article titled "Worlds in Confusion," Dr. Isaac Asimov, author of some 250 books of science and science fiction, attempted to deliver a witty coup de grace. Unlike editor John W. Campbell (who had helped to shape his own early career), Asimov went for the jugular vein, referring to Velikovsky as a "charlatan," a "madman," an "eccentric," a "cuckoo," a "nut," and a "screwball."

One of Velikovsky's most outspoken critics is Dr. Carl Sagan, the brilliant expert on planetary atmospheres and the glamorous chief of Cornell University's Department of Planetary Physics. Sagan, a NASA consultant and frequent guest on TV talk shows, is best known for designing the messages carried by the spaceprobes Pioneer 10 and Voyager into the depths of interplanetary and interstellar space. His credentials were impeccable. Velikovsky's were, to say the least, questionable. What right did a doctor (a psychiatrist, yet!) have to invade the sacred preserves of all the exact sciences with his baroque theories?

The scientists who formed the Committee for the Scientific Investigation of Claims of the Paranormal, have declared war on "all irrational, superstitious and obscurant" beliefs which block the path of true scientific progress. One can understand and truly appreciate the stated purposes of these sincere men (eight of the original group are Nobel laureates). Moreover, I admire and fully endorse their alleged objectives—to help eradicate ignorance, to expose charlatanry and fraud, to encourage clear thinking, to rid society of superstition and irrationality, and to encourage the use of the scientific method in our affairs and beliefs.

I believe in and subscribe to that—*except when, in pursuing these desirable goals, totalitarian methods are employed*. By this, I mean the refusal to discuss frankly and rationally that which they publicly condemn. I mean personal vilification. I mean character assassination. I mean conspiracy, elitism, or *any* collusion formed to smother ideas the Committee does not like or agree with—ideas against which the Committee previously sat in judgment. And I mean the use of intimidation to enforce the idiotic dogma that theirs is the only true and approved method by which anyone may pursue the truth about Nature's secrets.

When an elite group protected by a self-proclaimed cloak of infallibility vilifies, personally attacks, and intimidates a man championing a new theory or idea, it is no better than a gang. It is not invincible or infallible and should be exposed. In 1950 such a gang forced Immanuel Velikovsky's publisher to stop printing his book, *Worlds in Collision*. That gang succeeded with its pressure tactics because they were academics who wrote textbooks for that publisher, and therefore they had a lot of clout. Their cover story was that Velikovsky's theories were grievously in error and that he was a crackpot. The publisher caved in.

Nearly three decades later, the inheritors of the squeeze play continue the attack on the old man. His theories have all been proven wrong, they claim. He reshaped the chronology of ancient disasters to fit his pet ideas, they say. He's crazy, he's senile. It almost seems as though his very existence, like his crazy theories, "violates the laws of physics."

The truth is, they hate his *influence*. Velikovskiism has already eroded the carefully structured (and nurtured) laws of geologic uniformism, of long, uninterrupted stretches of time allowing evolution to have occurred so miraculously, so gradually, thus enabling *countless millions of forms* to adapt to the slowly changing environment.

That *would* require whole eons, entire epochs.

No doubt some of Velikovsky's ideas about what happened to the Earth and its inhabitants do violate our understanding of aspects of physics, thermodynamics, gravitation, and geologic processes. But so did the early fifteenth-century lectures of a certain student of Hieronymus Fabricius named Dr. William Harvey who, in 1616, was denounced for daring to contradict Galen and other great physiologists by claiming that the blood actually circulated throughout the body and that the heart was a muscular pump.

That seems rather odd in this enlightened day; we *should* have learned some of the lessons history teaches us about instantaneous negative reaction to new, unfamiliar ideas. Has even one of Velikovsky's detractors ever sincerely studied *the evidence in his favor*—without bias? Someone once grudgingly admitted that the psychiatrist had been right on the money too many times, and that maybe some of his material ought to be reexamined.

"No! He's completely wrong," cried one enemy, "and even when he's right, it's for all the wrong reasons." He later amended this stance, issuing a proclamation denouncing all of Velikovsky's correct predictions, "because they had all been anticipated by someone before him."

Velikovsky had the good sense to see all the disparate pieces of evidence when the eminent scientist hadn't a clue to their possible association. Could he have hated Velikovsky for crediting his sources and putting the evidence neatly together? Velikovsky's extensive bibliographies and references are there to be checked by anyone.

The cycles of the rise and fall of entire civilizations are empirical theory—also "without scientifically valid foundation." Nevertheless, the cycles stand—and demand explanation.

The members of the Committee for the Scientific Investigation of Claims of the Paranormal are indeed illustrious. So impressive are their credentials that the poor, ignorant layman is overwhelmed by the sheer power of their *opinion*—rather like Woody Allen timidly daring to question an illegal vote in a union hall full of angry dock workers hell bent on a strike.

No one we now recognize as a great inventor, true discoverer, or genius has ever belonged to any organization such as the Committee. The reason is simple. The men and women to whom we owe the very foundations of our civilization, science, law, art, and medicine *stood alone*. They were the *victims* of such gangs and were invariably "outsiders." Jenner, Semmelweiss, Galileo, and Pasteur head a long list of men who were right and thus oppressed by the majority of their peers (most of whom were either unfit or incapable of holding their exalted positions, and admitted it by attacking the only one who was).

Who remembers the names of those who hounded Ignatz Semmelweiss into a mental hospital, and finally into his grave? Semmelweiss was *saving* the lives of his patients by using preoperative antisepsis while all the other doctors were *killing* theirs.

The Committee for the Scientific Investigation of Claims of the Paranormal includes the most impressive lineup of brilliant scientific superstars on the contemporary scene. Who would dare risk a showdown with such an array of authorities? Hell, they must *know*. We don't. They're experts, leaders, trend-setters. Moreover, they're a solid phalanx with impeccable credentials.

To the Committee, astrology is *the* most offensive cult and must be eradicated. Of course, it is the most obvious target, so widespread and obviously ridiculous that the Committee fired its first broadside in 1975. It would have been just ginger-peachy—if at least one member of the Committee had ever mastered astrology or knew enough about it to subject it to scientific tests. But the scientists flatly refused to consider the hard statistical work of psychologist Vernon Clark, Michel Gauquelin, and many others who had made sincere, objective, and difficult studies of astrology—always at their own expense.*

During a special forum sponsored by the American Association for the Advancement of Science, Velikovsky was accused by Carl Sagan, in a critique that one witness described as a "57-page overkill," of making so many predictions that some of them were bound to prove correct. "My conclusion will be that where Velikovsky is original, he is very likely wrong; and that where he is right, the idea has been pre-empted by earlier workers."

Let's see about that. It happens that Velikovsky was both original *and* right about Venus's backward rotation, for one thing. Moreover, the history of astronomy, "as everyone knows," records enough crackpot ideas about Mars and Venus that were espoused by eminent scientists to make Velikovsky look positively conventional.

For example, one of the most illustrious astronomers during the first quarter of this century was Dr. William Henry Pickering of M. I. T. and Harvard fame. In a spectacular series of front-page stories in *The New York Times* during 1910, Dr. Pickering startled the world with his magnificently detailed personal "observations" of the inhabitants of the Red Planet hard at work building new canals. "The Martians are stopping at nothing to expand and fortify their great aqueducts," Pickering said. Forty years later, the "canals of Mars" concept was still pretty generally accepted.

But not by Velikovsky. "The surface of Mars will be found to be cratered like our Moon," he wrote in *Worlds in Collision*, "and so will the other inner

---

* See *Write Your Own Horoscope* (New York: New American Library, revised and updated edition, 1978).

planets." It's one of life's ironies that Dr. Pickering's reputation remains untarnished, while Velikovsky, who is *right*, is still damned as a crackpot.

Referring to the Noachian flood, Carl Sagan said, "It is clearly no use arguing against the catastrophic viewpoint that we have never seen such a catastrophe in our lifetime." We have never seen mountains raised or huge meteors crashing into the Earth either, but the evidence of such activity is accepted. As for the Deluge, Sir Charles Woolley's archaeological digs at Tel al Muquar, forty-five years ago, and elsewhere, proved the reality of the Flood.

Astronomers are, after all, human beings. A hundred of them can make ninety-nine wrong guesses about almost anything—the number of undiscovered planets, say—their mass, volume, orbital periods, right ascension, declination, and so on. But if a planet is discovered within ten million miles of the closest guess, a direct hit is claimed and another great "triumph" is chalked up for science. If the crackpots were given *that* much latitude, our space program might be run by little old ladies reading Ouija boards and tea leaves.

To my knowledge, no one before Velikovsky had ever suggested that Venus is the only planet in the solar system that rotates in a retrograde motion. Yet there's no cosmologic theory other than Velikovsky's to explain this mysterious backward rotation. James S. Pickering, a more contemporary astronomer, in *1001 Questions Answered About Astronomy* (New York: Grosset & Dunlap, 1959), wrote about Venus almost ten years *after* publication of *Worlds in Collision*: "The temperatures of its day side and its night side . . . do not offer the contrast which would exist *if Venus were like Mercury and kept the same side turned always to the Sun.* The surface temperature of the day side of Venus is about 150°F., while the temperature of the dark side is just a little below zero."*

---

* My italics. Pioneer II proved that Mercury rotated on its axis, while the temperature of Venus is now known to be about 800° F.

Such blatant boo-boos by the eminent Messrs. Pickering have never dulled their luster—at least not in the eyes of their colleagues.

This neither overlooks the apparent contradictions in Velikovsky's theory nor claims that he is invariably correct. However, the layman is constantly told by scientists that his ideas "violate the laws of conservation of energy and conservation of momentum." True—and Galileo's eccentric beliefs also violated church dogma, *which was wrong*. A strong suspicion seems to be surfacing in certain areas of science that the present understanding of some of these laws is due for a drastic overhaul. But even at the present stage of technological development such a revolution may be almost too shattering to contemplate. The medieval Church was the sole arbiter of what constituted both natural and "Divine" law. Imagine the turmoil if *those* holy gnostics could have had a glimpse of today's cosmology!

In his criticism of Velikovsky, Professor Sagan observed: "Science is self-correcting. The most fundamental axioms and conclusions may be challenged. The prevailing hypothesis must survive confrontation with observation."

It's true. This *is* what science says it is, and what science says it does. But you and I know, as do we all, that this isn't always so.

Science-baiter Charles Fort went a bit further in *The Book of the Damned*: "Science is like the Civil War in the U.S.A. No matter which side won, it would have been an American victory. By science, I mean the conventionalization of alleged enlightenment but when giving in there is not surrender, but partnership, and something that had been bitterly fought then becomes another factor in its, or her, prestige . . . science is a maw, or a headless and limbless stomach, an amoeba-like gut that maintains itself by incorporating the assimilable and rejecting the indigestible . . ."

As Isaac Asimov accurately observed, in addition to "sensing persecution from afar," two other characteristics of the real crackpot are (a) a morbid preoccupation with doom and disaster, and (b) the hint of having access to arcane knowledge. Velikovsky is anything *but* morbid about the implications of his work, and he flatly avoids occultism or even religion as dogma. His approach is that of a true scientist and real scholar.

It may be that many of his own supporters would be vastly relieved if scientific discovery and progress would totally and irrevocably erase the idea of catastrophism in historical times. We could then all get back to business as usual without the haunting worry about the stability of the solar system. It's unsettling to believe that the Sun may die, the Earth might slow down, wobble, slip off its axis, or even leave its orbit if approached too closely by some planetary maverick that changed the orderly structure of the solar system.

"There's no belief, however foolish," said Dr. Asimov in "Worlds in Confusion," *"that will not gather its faithful adherents who will defend it to the death."*

He's absolutely right, of course, but his put-down cuts both ways: the scientific establishment of yore has traditionally defended its views to the *other* guy's death. (Remember Semmelweis and Bruno?)

When the seventy-seven-year-old Velikovsky was invited to address a more liberalized forum of the AAAS, even the author's harshest critics were forced to admit that they had violated "the norms of science" and even common standards of decency in their treatment of him. But Dr. Norman Storer, a Baruch College sociologist, indulgently forgave the "human petulance" of the scientific community as being understandable because, after all, at the time (the early 1950s) the poor scientists were "threatened by McCarthyism on one hand and confronted by a man only marginally distinguished from a crackpot on the other."

Some alibi. However, even this obscure and anemic apology was mined with theoretical booby traps purportedly explaining why none of the things Velikovsky claims have happened to the Earth *could* have happened. All his dead-on hits are criticized as being "right for the wrong reasons" or are dismissed as "unoriginal."

Even if they are, it's difficult to understand and almost impossible to explain just how Velikovsky chose all those "unoriginal" ideas out of so many thousands of theories and put them together into a coherent and unified whole. He accurately postulated volcanic activity on the Moon, he said Mars had no canals but would be found to be heavily cratered, he stated that the Earth generates a huge magnetosphere (which, like Jupiter's, ought perhaps to be called the Van Allen-Velikovsky Belt), he predicted that Jupiter has a massively stronger magnetic field than the Earth's and would be found to be a powerful source of radio signals, and then predicted that Venus is a hot planet and would be found to be rotating in a retrograde motion.

Whether we accept Velikovsky's basic theory or not, it must be admitted that he came along at just the right time—at a most propitious and significant epoch in the history of science. The war was over, the world had entered the brightest and most promising period of scientific and technological gestation. We were on the threshold of the Space Age with all its wonders (including the specter of the hydrogen bomb). The climate was just right for Velikovsky.

By and large, the American and Soviet space probes have confirmed many of his postulates. (Of course, as a face-saving ploy, the scientific community might ascribe Velikovsky's "bizarre" theory to his remarkable clairvoyant gifts.) The exploration of space has fulfilled his fondest hopes, and he is now confident that future cosmic probes will completely vindicate him. "My work today is no longer theoretical," he told the AAAS forum. "Most of it is incorporated in textbooks and it doesn't matter whether credit is properly assigned."

He couldn't mean that, of course, not really. There must have been times when such callousness nearly broke his heart. Those who understand the colossal intellectual effort and dedication of this man find it difficult to maintain an objective frame of mind. It angered them to see this great figure humbled and dishonored for so many years. It was bad enough *before* we had the evidence from space exploration; at least then there was the excuse that no one had ever seen Mars or Mercury and didn't know much about Jupiter or Venus.

But *now?* This sort of treatment forces great minds into the crackpot mold. The fact that he does his best to discourage rancor and bitterness among his supporters is a measure of Velikovsky's character and integrity and is in sharp contrast to many of his critics who stoop to ridicule instead of presenting real evidence with objectivity, dispassion, reason, and courtesy.

Velikovsky has never abandoned hope of having his theory examined impartially; he has always carried himself with dignity and never reacted to (or imitated) the excesses of some of his persecutors. In fact, Velikovsky regards the attempt at repression of his ideas as nothing very unusual—just the latest in a long series of injustices heaped upon the true innovators and discoverers by the Big Science establishment.

He told me that he considers the pain of rejection he has endured as just "a manifestation of anxiety over an unwelcome truth . . . a motive is at play that may *appear* as scientific principle but which is wishful thinking. Those who lived in the sixteenth century didn't want to believe that the Earth was not the center of the Universe. Even much less does man wish to face the fact that he travels on a rock in space on a path that proved to be accident prone."

Nobody likes to be shown that the bedrock of nearly everything he believes in is nothing but brittle shale. Naturally Velikovsky was resisted; naturally his work is rejected. It would have been truly astonishing if he had received immediate scientific acceptance!

Carl Sagan observed, with characteristic aplomb, that many of Velikovsky's predictions "just flatly contradict physical laws." However, some of those "physical laws" have since been proven wrong.

There was a big hullabaloo in the mid-sixties when

the Soviet astronomer I. S. Shklovskii, in a co-authored book entitled *Intelligent Life in the Universe*, formulated a theory that the two moons of Mars were actually *artificial* satellites that were rocketed into orbit by the Martians a couple thousand years ago. This idea got its start in the early 1940s when a U.S. Naval Observatory astronomer calculated the orbits of Mars's two moons, Phobos and Diemos, and concluded that they were moving closer to their primary planet. Much, much later, this was found to be wrong. Nevertheless, on the basis of these figures, Shklovskii collaborated with an American astronomer to develop the most exotic theory since Pickering enchanted the world with his eyewitness reports of Martians building their canals. (Science wasn't very self-correcting that time; Dr. Pickering's pre-1920s observations were *confirmed* by two equally eminent astronomers!)

And who, you might wonder, was the American astronomer who collaborated with Shklovskii? You guessed it—*none other than the director of Cornell's Laboratory for Planetary Studies—Carl Sagan.*

During an interview on the Tonight Show, the same Professor Sagan casually told host Johnny Carson about the false "Mars-moons-are-space-cities" myth and explained how he worked with NASA to change Mariner's trajectory so that its cameras could be trained on the mysterious Mars moons from close up in order to settle the question of their real nature once and for all.

"There were, of course, no cities," Sagan said coolly. "In fact the pictures of Phobos looked something like a pockmarked potato." That seemed to be that. No big triumph for science, just another crackpot theory shot down by self-correcting scientific research—*and* a fantastically good job of space technology.

At no point, did Sagan give the slightest indication on that televised show that he had been the co-author of that most interesting theory.

Both Velikovsky and Sagan (and presumably *everyone* who seeks scientific truth) obtain their data from basically similar sources. However, this enormous mass of data is processed through our personal, often subjective computers, and therein lies the bone of contention. Dr. Sagan is genuinely liked and respected as a sincerely good man and a brilliant all-around scientist. But no one is omniscient. And, in fact, using the criteria of Isaac Asimov, Sagan *himself* (in the eyes of many envious colleagues) qualifies as a bona-fide crackpot.

The "scientific method" works only when it is applied objectively and dispassionately. The initial greeting and subsequent handling of Velikovsky's theories have reflected anything *but* dispassion, the main reason probably being that Velikovsky is an "outsider," as is often the case with real discoverers.

It is not hard to predict what the reaction to the telemetered pictures of Phobos and Diemos would have been had Velikovsky, and *not* Sagan, been the co-author of *Intelligent Life in the Universe*.

Before making generalizations about crackpots, perhaps it is best to consider the question from different angles. John Campbell once asked a visitor, "How do you go about convincing a thick-headed conservative that he's an obstacle to progress?" After a respectable period of frowning, lip-chewing, and squinting quizzically at the ceiling to see if the answer might be up there, his visitor finally allowed as how he didn't know.

"You CAN'T!" Campbell said triumphantly. "Any more than you can convince a real soft-headed liberal that he has jelly for a brain." Which simply demonstrates that what is "perfectly obvious" to us is sheer gibberish to the other dunce.

General Haig, who represented the Army on the Pentagon's Joint Chiefs of Staff, is an educated, intelligent, capable, and apparently rational human being. But during some close questioning by a reporter who was trying to correlate the Nazi war crimes of World War II with some American atrocities in Vietnam, his rationality somehow failed him. Having established the guilt of the German generals for obeying inhuman orders, the reporter asked, "If you had received an order from the President to bomb neutral Cambodian villages which you knew were filled with thousands of women and children, would you pass on the order to conduct such raids?"

Considering the implication of the question, Haig was in trouble no matter what his answer was.

After a short pause, General Haig calmly replied, "Yes," and proceeded to explain: "If you read my commission you'd see that I'm bound to obey the orders of the Commander in Chief of the armed forces or any duly constituted official..."

To be fair, General Haig made it clear that to him it was totally inconceivable that such an order would ever be issued. In retrospect, considering who was President at the time, it boggles the mind. We are indeed a strange species; it seems almost a miracle that we've managed to survive on this planet so far without destroying it or ourselves. If the President *had* issued such a command, General Haig's sworn commission would require him to carry out orders that he *admits* are morally abhorrent.

To a limited degree, this kind of military mentality exists in all of us, scientist and layman alike. Controlled scientific tests have proved that many people will inflict pain, torture—even death on another human being when ordered to by someone "in authority." The exercise of logic and/or reason can be completely blocked by a preconditioned attitude (which the *blockee* cannot see), whatever its persuasion. "Eyes have they and they will not see; ears have they and they will not hear."

There's a growing mountain of evidence that something is wrong with our relatively short history when it is compared to *at least* several million years of our existence as a species. Yet science persistently and adamantly strives to discredit Velikovsky's catastrophism rather than reexamine its own dearly cherished beliefs, mainly the bizarre idea that humankind was little more than an animal just 20,000 or 30,000 years ago.

Yet some surprisingly "modern" scientific findings

were common knowledge in ancient times. For example, Dr. William Harvey's theory of the circulation of the blood was apparent to badly wounded men (and those who cared for them) in wars waged for thousands of years nearly everywhere on Earth. Early Hindu physicians recognized the fact that the blood circulated.

The ancient Greeks knew that the Earth is a spheroid, a planet just like the other "wanderers" in the night sky, and that it revolves around the Sun (not vice versa) in a generally easterly direction. The fate of Giordano Bruno, Galileo, and the "heretics" who tried to prove otherwise shows that this and other knowledge went into complete eclipse during the next millennium.

Hardly anyone has defended Velikovsky by pointing out that if much of our highly advanced scientific learning was common knowledge thousands of years ago, perhaps the fact that ancient people all over the world believed that various World Ages ended with almost cyclic cataclysms destroying virtually all traces of civilization lends credence to his theories. It is difficult to imagine how isolated Polynesians or Australian aborigines, for example, could have known about the existence of great civilizations if there had been none for them to see or know—even through hearsay.

According to other legends, these destructions were caused by the Sun, Jupiter (Zeus), and Venus (Pallas Athene). Velikovsky used a different name—"Typhon." It was, he says, still *another* name for Venus and the "battle" she waged with Jupiter. According to Apollodorus, the summit of mountainous Thrace was called Haemus because of the "stream of blood" which gushed out of the mountain "when the heavenly battle was fought between Zeus and Typhon and Typhon was struck by a thunderbolt..."

The terrified witnesses of the battle between Zeus and Typhon named the Egyptian shore of the Red Sea Typhonia. In his *History of Herodotus*, G. Rawlinson wrote: "Typhon, which was a dragon, when struck by the bolts of lightning, fled in search of an underground hideaway. Not only did he cut furrows in the Earth and form the beds of rivers, but descending underground, he made fountains break forth."

Rawlinson also wrote, "The Earth was submerged in the ocean but was drawn by Tefaafanau," according to the Polynesians of Paumotu. "These new islands were bated by a star." In the month of March, the Polynesians celebrate the god Taafanua. In Arabic, Tyfoon is a whirlwind and Tufan is the Deluge. In Chinese the same word appears as Ty-fong.

In the second book of his *Natural History*, Pliny writes, "A terrible comet was seen by the people of Ethiopia and Egypt, to which Typhon, the king of that period, gave his name; it had a fiery appearance and was twisted like a coil, and it was very grim to behold; it was not really a star so much as what might be called a ball of fire."

And according to the translations of the Text of Taoism, "The breath of heaven was out of harmony, and the four seasons do not observe their proper time ... the sky and the Earth resounded, mountains and hills were moved and loud did the firmament roar, and the huge earth groaned" when Zeus lashed Typhon with his mighty bolts.

"Legendary myth," says orthodox science. "Utter nonsense." Yet catastrophism has never been *dis*-proven.

Velikovsky says that Typhon was a comet that ran against the Earth, but was the *same* as Pallas Athene: "In the long battle of the celestial bodies, one of them made the world entirely dark, disfigured creation, and filled it with vermin." As described by Apollodorus and others, "Typhon spread like an animal over the sky with its many heads and winged body, with fire flaming from its mouths."

However, we need not rely on ancient history, sacred writings, *or* the "known" physical laws to make a case for catastrophism. Velikovsky himself didn't make much of a case from the existence of the asteroid belt, that ring of debris orbiting between Mars and Jupiter, or how it may be connected with

Jupiter's great red spot. But another group of scientists at Columbia, after a computer study, concluded that no planet could *possibly* have originated closer to the Sun than the orbit of Jupiter. Still—the existence of Mercury, Venus, Earth, and Mars had to be explained.

They did it by postulating that only the "gas giants" are truly primitive bodies. All the smaller, inner planets must, therefore, have resulted from the *repeated* disruptions of Jupiter.

Velikovsky is quite explicit about the birth of Venus, i.e., by eruption from Jupiter. But he has never speculated about the *cause* of Jupiter's erratic behavior. And since there has never, to my knowledge, been much debate about the actual age of the asteroid belt or how it was formed, let's examine an even more exotic notion than Velikovsky's.

Astronomers have no difficulty conceptualizing exploding stars or even *entire galaxies* that destroy themselves—as long as they're far enough away. Supernovae are eventually re-formed into the heavy material from which younger stars will reincarnate. But what about the debris of a destroyed *planet*?

Nowhere in astronomical literature is there any theory to explain how planets can become unstable, stop rotating, alter their axes of inclination, leave their orbits, or (God forbid) blow *themselves* up. Only in science fiction are stars or planets ever destroyed by the tampering of "intelligent" Beings.

Still . . . we have the new "object Kowal" orbiting between Jupiter and Saturn, and the asteroid belt out there to explain. It's not the simple, neat ring of evenly distributed stuff most of us learned about in school. These large planetoids—many of them hundreds of times bigger than the moons of Mars—actually streak in as far as the Earth. The "minor planets" Apollo and Adonis, for example, have been hurled into orbits that lie between Venus and the Sun, while Icarus comes even closer to the Sun than Mercury! Asteroid Hidalgo sweeps in a great ellipse almost as far as Saturn's orbit. The small asteroid

Hermes has been calculated to be able to swing between the Earth and the Moon.

All this suggests that the asteroid belt was given a stupendous initial "kick" to send this much stuff whirling off in all directions around the solar system.

As we've seen here, Velikovsky effectively uses folklore, myth, and legend to support some of his heterodox contentions. Can his study of ancient legends be extrapolated to include the asteroid belt? He seems to have given short shrift to the possibility that Typhon—a fierce and powerful entity in Greek legend—is *not* Pallas Athene or Venus, but *a destroyed planet*!

In legend, Typhon is often identified with and even called the son of Typhoeus, a many-headed monster and father of the Harpies. His counterpart in Hebrew legend is Rahab—also a monster, something like a dragon.

Suppose an awesome cosmic event—triggered by a huge solar upheaval—actually did knock a planet-sized chunk out of Jupiter, as Velikovsky says? That cataclysm could have resulted in the explosion of an entire world—an event so stupendous that ancient people would refer to it in their histories, which we dismiss as mere legend.

If such a pre-asteroid belt planet happened to be conjunct (or almost conjunct) Jupiter when something went wrong—perhaps a terrible nuclear conflagration on Typhon—Jupiter would certainly have felt the effect of such a blast. Being a gas giant, Jupiter could have reacted in *exactly* the way Velikovsky described.

No matter which crackpot theory is formulated for the asteroid belt, some day one of them is going to be proven true!

CHAPTER 9

Who Goes There?

In many ways the 1950s were closer to the days of World War I than to the 1970s and 1980s. For example, no intelligent film maker today would dream of taking the finest science fiction story ever written (virtually the unanimous conclusion of s-f afficionados and the best-known authors of the genre) and turning it into a turkey called *The Thing*, but in the 1950s that's what happened.

John W. Campbell, the author of that chilling yarn (and if you haven't read "Who Goes There?" not only do I heartily recommend it, I envy your adventure) was a young MIT and Duke University-trained physicist who, during the late 1930s, was writing under the pseudonym of Don A. Stuart.

Campbell went on to become editor of *Astounding Stories* and within thirty-five years, single-handedly revolutionized pulp science fiction and transformed it into its now "respectable" literary form. He personally coaxed, prodded, teased, cajoled, and successfully trained just about every science fiction writer of importance in the field—names like Robert Heinlein, Isaac Asimov, A. E. Van Vogt, Lester Del Rey, Lewis Padgett, Raymond F. Jones, P. Schuyler Miller, Eric Frank Russell, Ben Bova, and scores of others. Although Campbell inherited the mantles of Jules Verne, H. G. Wells, and Hugo Gernsbach, he outdid them all with his insistence that science fiction must be more than spinning well-plotted yarns of pure fantasy.

The stories he paid for had to be logical, compelling extrapolations of known, hard science, and God help the neophyte who couldn't or wouldn't learn the philosophical and engineering structure of a Campbell-style story. The first one Isaac Asimov managed to sell him had been turned down (with generous, detailed coaching) by Campbell *eighteen* times, *which may help explain the good Dr. Asimov's prodigal prolificacy.*

After changing the content and format of the best-known s-f magazine, Campbell changed the title to *Analog*—Science Fiction—Science Fact, the perennially acknowledged "aristocrat" of science fiction magazines. Once when he received a long futuristic tale of alien invasion, catastrophe, and hopelessness, Campbell, who personally read everything that crossed his desk, dictated this characteristically terse response: "Okay, bub. You've stated the problem. Now solve it."

Many of his writers were top scientists, as were some of his more illustrious readers. Albert Einstein was one of Campbell's early subscribers, and at the other end of the political spectrum, Wernher von Braun had copies of *Astounding Stories* smuggled through Sweden during World War II to the German rocket base at Peenemünde.

Campbell was always a scientific spoiler who loved to bash brains with the top experts in any field whatsoever, whether it was an established science or something as unorthodox as dowsing or astrology. He was one of the first to suggest that the Sun and many other stars emitted an as-yet-undetected, unknown force, and he had some rather unique ideas about the relationship of man to God, as you'll learn at the end of the following interview.

Any of his writers would swear that an editorial session with Campbell was like going through a meat-grinder. "I wasn't too popular as a kid," he once observed. "In fact I was a spoilsport in the neighborhood because I treated everything as a problem—and solved it." (Campbell was equally unpopular with people who regarded his gratuitous self-evaluations as those of an egotistical maniac. He was, in fact, both healthily egotistic and profoundly humble.) He ruined hide-and-seek for all the kids he played with by organizing the standard naval-search pattern—a spiral moving out from the center. "That loused up hide-and-seek," he grinned ruefully, shrugging his brawny shoulders. "It simply wasn't a game anymore."

Author Harry Harrison, who put together a book of Campbell's offbeat, iconoclastic editorials, opened his Introduction thus: "When I was fifteen years old I thought John W. Campbell was God." Harrison wasn't the only one. In every issue of *Analog* Campbell devised impossible-to-put-down editorials on just about every subject under, in, on, and beyond the Sun. As Harrison said, they were "idiosyncratic, personal, prejudiced, far-reaching, annoying and sabotaging" as hell. Altogether, they probably comprise one of the most addictive, refreshingly sane, thoroughly enjoyable literary and intellectual pursuits available.

The technique of his editorial Inquisition was as frustrating for some writers as an early Greek's attempt to deal with Socrates. "It is also," said Harry Harrison, "like being fed through a buzz saw. I can vouch for that because a Campbell conversation consists almost entirely of loaded questions that demand answers. No one really likes to be forced to think. Campbell forces you."

This may be one reason why there has always been an enormous cross-over readership between *Analog* and most other scientific and technical journals. Certainly the best film and television science fiction is patterned on Campbell-style stories. He seems to have almost *created* our future! Those who still have copies of *Astounding* from the late 1930s and early 1940s can review a remarkable series of highly accurate prophesies. Campbell wasn't too happy with that view: "Science fiction has been entirely too conservative," he complained.

But he kept the pot boiling. In one of his provocative dissertations he wrote: "Editorially, I shall continue to try to investigate the nature of the stuffing in any suspiciously bulging shirts around. My business is directly concerned with the progress and achievement of the human race; any orthodoxy that tends to sidetrack or otherwise impede progress is interfering with my business, and I'll do what I can to sabotage them."

Campbell was less interested in scientific theory than with workable engineering. He stormed into every sacred scientific preserve, all guns firing, and printed straight scientific articles on such brain-busters as the Dean Drive, a device that violates all known principles of motion and gravitation, and the Hieronymus Machine, another esoteric (patented, incidentally) contrivance that, when you build it, generates and broadcasts an unknown energy or force that has been reliably reported to influence—even kill—living creatures from far away. Campbell once provided the technical information for a writer named Cleve Cartmill to do a story about an atom bomb. It described and depicted (with illustrations) an almost exact replica of the "fat boy" atom bomb that was eventually dropped on Japan. Naturally, the FBI and security police at the Manhattan Project figured there was a leak; they pounced on Campbell's office only to discover that atomic bombs had been his stock-in-trade for several years. He freely predicted fifteen years in advance that a hydrogen bomb would be the next evolutional step in military hardware. If the AEC had read Campbell's forecast, it could have saved a fortune in taxpayers' money. The Russians used lithium hydride, as Campbell had predicted; their test cost about $20 million. Our scientific experts "proved mathematically" that lithium hydride could not possibly work; we developed a hydrogen bomb all right—at a cost of about $3 *billion*! Later, the United States switched to lithium hydride.

In one of his editorials, Campbell wrote: "Human beings are so highly complex that, to date, no one of them has ever succeeded in figuring out (a) what he is, (b) what he wants, (c) where he's been, or (d) where he's going. . . ."

Top officials in the space program and two generations of bright young scientists (many of whom are now NASA officials, astronauts, astronomers, inventors and innovators) kept a close watch on the working of John W. Campbell's brain.

The following interview with John Campbell was printed in *Science & Mechanics*, February, 1968.

Question: You've piloted *Analog* through World War II and into the space age. How does this time in history differ from your expectations thirty years ago?

Campbell: We had general ideas as to which way things were going, but no specific ideas as to just when. Harry Stein did an article for us some years ago called "Science Fiction Is Too Conservative," pointing out that most of the things that we now have were in stories predicted to happen around 1990 or the year 2010—something like that. Spaceships to the Moon? Oh, they were going to be along around 1980 or 1990, and so on. We are *much* too conservative.

Question: A statement in your recently published book of editorials goes that you consider part of your job to do all you can to sabotage "any suspiciously bulging shirts around." What do you mean by that?

Campbell: There always has been and always will be stuffed shirts in any business. Unfortunately a highly respected stuffed shirt can do more to impede progress than the most determined man of ill will. For instance, the Church Fathers who opposed Galileo were men of great learning and good will. They certainly did a great deal to sabotage him. It is always the men of good will and the stuffed shirts who do most to impede human progress.

Question: You've pioneered a whole new kind of science fiction and set the style for this medium. What would you like to be doing if you weren't editor of a science fiction magazine?

Campbell: I'd start one. Look, this has been my

hobby since I was a freshman at MIT. I am one of those fortunate individuals who has somehow gotten other people to pay him for enjoying his hobby. You know, that's very habit forming.

Question: What's the formula for keeping the old *Astounding* and now *Analog* around as the aristocrats of science fiction?

Campbell: That's very simple. We don't have a formula. This is an entertainment medium. The entertainment business is the most unstable business of all human affairs . . . You know, "There's no business like show business?" Basically a magazine is show business. If you have a formula, then people know what to expect and they've read that book. If you don't have a formula, then they haven't finished reading the book yet. Perhaps my guidance philosophy is expressed in Kipling's "Rhyme of the *Mary Glouster*."

"They copied all they could follow, but they couldn't copy my mind, so I left them sweating and stealin', a year and a half behind."

Only when you are thinking up things that they aren't quite ready to think up themselves will they follow your magazine.

Question: What don't you like about science, or I should say, the "scientific method?"

Campbell: I think the scientific method is fine, but I am reminded of George Bernard Shaw's comment when somebody asked him what he thought of Christianity. He said, "I think it's a noble doctrine. It's too bad that no one has tried it in the last 2,000 years." It would be a great idea if the scientists would actually use the method they claim they use, to determine by experiment, by testing, instead of deciding, "Well, that can be shown mathematically that it is pure nonsense. It's *impossible* . . ."

Question: Can you give me an example?

Campbell: Yes. Shortly after I got my degree in physics, I was sitting on my front porch and I saw a ball of lightning form in the field just across the road from me. I watched that ball bounce gently over the tops of the grasses, bounce off the side of a barn, go over and explode an eight-inch tree into oak toothpicks. The next time I was visiting back at MIT, I went to see my physics professor. He *assured* me it was physically impossible for a ball of lightning to exist, that no competent observer had ever reported the phenomena, and that there was mathematical *proof* of its impossibility! That's fine. As far as I could make out, what constituted a reliable observer, a competent observer, was one who *didn't* report it. The fact of reporting it *proved* you were incompetent because they *knew* it was impossible! Of course, now we know a little more. Now we have an explanation. You see, a ball of lightning is nothing but a plasmoid. Now this can be generated by such and such a phenomenon. Now that they have a theory, they will accept evidence. Until they had the theory, all evidence was rejected.

Question: When the Manhattan Project was top secret, you ran a yarn that allegedly contained the formula for the atomic bomb. What *really* happened then?

Campbell: The formula for the atomic bomb—that doesn't quite describe it. A newspaperman by the name of Cleve Cartmill, a science fiction writer for some years, had a plot idea for a story involving an atomic bomb. Now, atomic bombs, atomic weapons, and atomic power plants had been stock-in-trade in science fiction since H. G. Wells was writing his stuff at the turn of the century. Well, Cleve sent in the query, he wanted to do the story about the atomic bomb, but how do you *set off* an atomic bomb? What sort of a fuse mechanism do you use? Do you have a little cyclotron in it or what? I wrote back and told him that (from what was then known) it would be set off by combining subcritical masses into a single supercritical mass which would cause the chain reaction. So Cleve wrote the story—his description of the atomic bomb. I bought the yarn, sent it out to an artist to illustrate. We published it . . . and the Pentagon blew its stack even though it was sheer coincidence. The artist had just drawn an illustration, you know. He had no information, but that illustration happened to be an almost *perfect* match for the design of the "fat boy" bomb which was then being designed and worked on at Los Alamos! Moreover, the description of the explosion of an atomic bomb in that story was more accurate than anything that was published until after the Smythe Report came up. Well, military intelligence was around, and then I learned one additional factor that had them upset. It happened that Cleve Cartmill, the author, lived in an area in California close to where a number of the young physicists of the Manhattan Project lived. And the M.I. was very much afraid that some physicist had been shooting off his mouth in a bar and Cleve had overheard him. They questioned Cleve about it. Fortunately, Cleve still had the letter in which I had written him the description of the atomic bomb probabilities. The M.I. then came around to see me. I was able to say that I had gotten the information from the *Physical Review* for June 15, 1940.

Question: Most of today's top writers of science fiction started out as stablemates in *Astounding Stories*—Isaac Asimov, Willy Ley, Robert Heinlein. When you have editorial conferences, are they really the meat-grinders you're accused of conducting?

Campbell: I don't know. It's awfully hard for the meat-grinder to tell whether it's a meat-grinder or not. Maybe. What happens is we have bull sessions. Usually, there's more than two involved. I like to throw out hard questions and see what they can come up with. Obviously, what we want are unexpected solutions because the expected solutions don't make good stories.

Question: Since you're in the business of scientific prophesy, what do think the chances are of eventually building a truly sophisticated computerized robot—one possessing self-awareness?

Campbell: My present feeling is that we'll have a computer capable of self-awareness by 1975.[*] This will not be a robot in the usual "tin woodsman" concept. There's no reason why a machine should be made like a man. A man, his shape, his whole function, evolved in a wild universe, a wild world in which he had to be able to do everything for himself. The very concept of a machine civilization implies that there are specialized talents and specialized devices available. There's *no reason* why a machine would have to do everything for itself . . . Incidentally, I have a functional robot in my home now—and *have* had for about sixteen years. This robot has one finger stuck up in the living room to feel the temperature of the air. It has another finger in the boiler to see whether there's enough water, and another one tells whether or not the temperature is high enough. It's called an automatic oil burner furnace. This is a true, single-function robot. Another type of single-function robot is your freezer. It automatically turns on whenever the temperature in your freezer compartment gets too high and turns off when it's low enough. Those are all robots. And certainly your modern dial telephone is a robot. But none of them is the "tin man" type. We *will* have a thinking robot in about seven years.

Question: What's the best current estimate for intelligent life existing on the nearby solarian planets?

Campbell: On the solar planets the probability is a good approximation of zero . . . on the other

---

[*] He was several years off on this one. It happened in 1972—a year after he died.

planets of our solar system, very low indeed. If there were intelligent life on Venus, it could not be life as we know it. Therefore, we have no clues to it whatever. Jupiter is too big, too gaseous, and too cold. Again, it couldn't be life as we know it. The planets farther out are *so* cold that chemical reactions would not make life possible—*life as we know it*. Now, if you want to talk about *Beings of pure force, or Entities of pure psyche, I don't know, maybe they can live in the Sun*, but I don't know anything about them.

Question: There's a lot of new speculation about prehistoric visitations from other worlds. Do you know of any evidence or theory to support this idea?

Campbell: Let's put it this way! If it's prehistoric, that means there would be no solid evidence. If it *is* evidence, then we call it history. Now, one of the problems in interpreting old material is that we don't have the background of experience they had. We don't understand their idiomatic phrases and they wouldn't understand ours. I think one of the most magnificent examples of the confusion of the idiomatic phrase is the tale of Jonah and the whale. According to the Bible, there was a storm at sea and the sailors decided that Jonah was a "Jonah." He was a jinx and they threw him into the sea and "Jonah was in a great fish." Now it just happens that the original manuscript from which that was translated was done in Aramaic, and the Aramaic idiom for "in a great fish" can properly be translated into English as "in a terrible stew," so what *really* happened was that Jonah was thrown overboard and was in a terrible stew. When you translate an idiom—*literally*—you can reach some very peculiar conclusions. Ezekiel saw the flaming wheel. Fine! You can get into some very interesting arguments discussing the Book of Ezekiel and suggesting that he really did see an extraterrestrial visitor. Well, if we moderns with all our radar, telescopes, instantaneous radio communication, and jet pursuit planes—if *we* can't determine whether or not there are flying saucers, I'd want to be *damned* sure of any reports I received from prehistory.

Question: How do you classify the difference between science, truth, logic and/or reason?

Campbell: All right. "Truth" is an abstract concept of the Universe. The proposition is: "There is Truth." The business of science is the effort to find those truths. As one of my friends, Dr. Wayne Batteau, put it, "The Universe is full of information; man's job is to read it out." There is also information stored in a magnetic tape. If you know just how to go about it, you can read it out. The Universe is *full* of information. If we can just figure out how to devise a "Universe tape recorder" which can read out that information, that's science. Logic is a formalized system of manipulating postulates to reach a conclusion. *Mathematics* is logic. You say, "Let A or X equal the unknown." Now you go through this system of manipulations and reach the conclusion that $X = 17.3$. That is logic. But I can also give you another example of *perfect* logic; and believe it or not, this is perfect and faultless: *If* the Moon is made of green cheese, and there's a cheese shortage in Switzerland, then we should bring pieces of the Moon down to Switzerland. It's *nuts*! But it's logic. The only thing wrong with it is that the postulates are false. I have talked to an individual who is more perfectly logical than any *sane* man I've ever encountered. She was a psychotic paranoid, *completely* insane. She had a set of convictions, including the idea that she was being persecuted by telepaths who were reading her mind, and they were giving her a terrible time. And her logic is absolutely faultless—*if* you accept that there are telepaths around, and *if* you accept that they were ill-disposed toward her . . . then everything she said followed logically. Reason, on the other hand, has to do with the selection of postulates that *work*! This woman was *logical*—but she wasn't reasonable. Many people fail dismally to distinguish between logic and reason. A psychotic paranoid (of the type psychologists call a "computing psychotic") thinks like a computing machine. Computing machines are *completely* irrational. They'll do the nuttiest things imaginable *because* they're logical. Put in just one false postulate and they'll carry it out with *absolutely* blind and faultless logic . . . to their destruction and yours, most likely. I think it might be a good idea to put up—by every automatic computer, every computing machine—a sign reading: "I Will Do What You Say, Not What You Mean."

Question: There's a huge gap between the orbits of Mars and Jupiter where another planet might easily be postulated. Instead, there's the asteroid belt, an area of rocklike or meteoric debris. What's the explanation for this?

Campbell: All I can say is that I don't have a direct line to God. I don't know, but I've observed *one* thing with interest and amusement . . . numerology, whatever you want to call it: there are no five-sided or pentagonal crystals. There are atomic isotopes of all weights from one up to, oh . . . two hundred and sixty—*except* for atomic weight five. *If* there were a planet there, it would be the fifth planet. Maybe five is an unstable factor in the Universe.

Question: Another large mass of debris or rubble orbits sixty degrees behind the Moon. There are also craters on the Moon and Mars. Are these phenomena related?

Campbell: The most recent work on that mass of rubble following the Moon indicates a question as to whether it is a mass or rubble or a cloud of very, very fine dust. Apparently it's an optical phenomenon having to do with what is known as the zodiacal light or the *gegenschein*.

The Earth has its rings, much like Saturn. But of course, being down in the middle of them we don't see them. It's apparently a fine dust, but there are certain angles at which it can be observed, if sunlight hits it just right, and so forth. Apparently that's what was seen and mistakenly identified in what is known as "the Trojan Position" with respect to the Moon.

Question: You are known to give serious consideration to any real subject, however unorthodox it might seem. How do you deal with the kooks and crackpots who must inevitably beat a path to your wide-open door?

Campbell: It's the old problem. You have to select and distinguish the crackpots from the geniuses. There's only one sure test of the difference between a crackpot and a genius: a genius is a crackpot who makes money at it. A genius, in other words, is simply a man whose idea sounded crazy—until he *demonstrated* that it really worked and was, therefore, economically practical. You know, when Henry Ford was trying to set up the original Ford Motor Company (that was before he decided he hated New York bankers and Wall Street brokers) he tried to get some money here in New York and the bankers he approached hired some engineers to examine his proposal. They were told that that "planetary transmission" idea he had was completely impractical. It wouldn't work. It would fall apart. It had to break down. Ford was a crackpot, but he eventually proved to be a genius. My problem here is to figure out, *before* they have made money at it, which ones who come here are the crackpots and which are true geniuses.

Question: Science fictioneers have written about time travel for decades. Now it is a subject for the movies and television. *Assuming* that time travel will eventually occur, what kind of laws or rules would you anticipate to govern the phenomenon?

Campbell: You might say, "None." They simply don't pay enough attention to it to offer any resistance to the idea. You get more of a fight on something like my interest in the psi faculties. ESP is one aspect of psi. But I can't use the term ESP because I'm also interested in levitation—the ability to float in the air—teleportation, telekinesis, and so forth. This isn't sensory perception; it is extramuscular activity. So by combining the two unusual talents, we call it "psi." The scientists are absolutely *sure* that nothing of that sort is possible: "It's all silly superstition, nonsense." They won't even deign to test such "nonsense." At the same time, the engineering field crews are using one form of ESP known as dowsing. Not to find well water, but to find the pipes they have to fix—pipes buried under the street here somewhere. Oh sure—they have these electromagnetic gadgets that are supposed to find pipes—*metal* pipes—provided there's no metal in the way. But suppose you're a plumber who has to fix one of these polyvinyl chloride plastic pipes? You can't find one of these with a metal detector. Suppose you're a plumber who has to fix a cast-iron sewer pipe that runs somewhere under a steel-reinforced concrete floor? All the metal detector will find are the criss-crossing metal rods in the concrete. At this point they put their fancy electronic gadget away and pull out a pair of dowsing rods and go find the pipe. But *scientists* won't look at that: "Oh, that doesn't happen! It's nonsense, it's superstition, it's *folklore*! That *proves* it's no good."

Question: Let's *assume* that time travel will eventually occur. What kind of laws or rules would you anticipate to govern the phenomenon?

Campbell: Oh, brother. I can't do any coherent thinking on that subject until you give me some suggestion of the principles on which time travel works. For example: if you have a time machine capable of going back into the past, then comes the interesting question of what happens if I go back and prevent Lincoln's assassination? That changes history as we know it. But *I am a product* of the history we know. If Lincoln were *not* assassinated, I might have had another great-grandfather, in which case I would not be *me* and I wouldn't be here. Therefore, I wouldn't be able to travel backward in time to prevent the assassination of Lincoln. So it didn't happen anyway. In time travel you have entirely too many involuted paradoxes . . . if you assume *that* sort of time travel to the past, without giving a much more comprehensive analysis or postulate structure to work on. Now if you assume that every time there's a shift in history a whole new Universe springs from that shift, this means that if you go back into the past and see someone walking down the street back in 1930 and talk to him, you've changed something—caused a shift in history—and you therefore cannot get back to your starting point. Because, you see, you've changed history. Your starting point isn't *there* anymore.

Question: There are a staggering number of life forms now existing on our own planet. Will there be an equally rich ecology on any world where life is found?

Campbell: The chances are that the answer is "yes," except that we may find life on a world that is still very primitive—one that hasn't evolved to the level of complexity Earth has reached. But the basis of my saying "yes" is this: Australia was isolated by oceans from the rest of the continents of the planet for an *enormously* long period. In Australia there evolved a whole line of marsupial mammals. They're not the true placental mammals, they're marsupials. Among them was the Tasmanian wolf. I saw one and it looked exactly like a wolf except that it had very heavy hindquarters, and the tail, instead of being of almost uniform diameter for its full length, was thick and heavy at the base and tapered toward its end. It was a close relative of the kangaroo: it was a marsupial. But it looked exactly like a wolf; it had the same kind of jaws, the same kind of teeth. Its legs were very similar in muscular design throughout. In a continental area where there are large herbivorous mammals, *some* creature will evolve to prey on those herbivores. If you have a fast-running herbivore such as the kangaroo, you need some kind of carnivorous mammal that can run as fast and as long as they can. So, in an ecological system, you will develop a cursorial carnivorous animal. Well, the Tasmanian wolf has evolved. For many, many millions of years South America was isolated from North America but was connected by land bridges to Australia. During this period, South America had a marsupial evolution very much like Australia's. Over geological epochs these land bridges broke. South America became isolated from Australia. And then a land bridge, the Isthmus of Panama to North America, formed where the placental mammals had evolved. The placental mammals moved into South America along the Isthmus. Very shortly, there were no more marsupial carnivores in South America. The placental mammals were more efficient. Wherever there is an ecological niche, an entity will evolve to fill that niche. When two ecologies come into contact like that, the one with the more efficient niche-filler will take over. That's what happened to the Tasmanian wolf. When men moved dogs into Australia, the Tasmanian wolf vanished from Australia.

Question: What's behind the current youth revolution, with its retreat from conformism, its escape into psychedelic drugs and hatred for the Establishment?

Campbell: Um-hum. The old business of the Straw Man. When you are going to rebel against something, you pick the most extreme examples of its particular aspect and claim that those extreme examples are *typical* of what you're rebelling against. That is, if you are going to rebel against labor unions, for instance. (Instead of capitalism, I'm going to rebel against labor unions.) Well, labor unions "as everybody knows," are made up of goon squads that beat people to death, and of crooked labor bosses who steal the union funds and ruin the benefits of union workers. You *can* cite court cases of such people. What you're doing is choosing the *worst* examples and claiming they are typical. This is perfectly standard operational procedure; now as far as the so-called hippies with psychedelic drugs and so forth are concerned—yeah—the young people of today are out of communication. They resent it. But picture a group of adults at a gathering or party—discussing a football game or a party they attended last night, having a fine sociable time—and a three-year-old child is in the room and getting no attention. He *tries* to get attention, but everyone is so busy talking: just, ah, "Not now dear." You've seen that sort of situation? Well, presently Junior just sort of stands back, looks around at Mama and Aunt Mary or Uncle Joe and goes over, hauls back his foot and —whap! He *gets* attention! Su-u-r-r-e—he gets spanked for it, but at least they're paying *attention* to him! These hippies are trying to get someone to pay attention to them . . . to make them feel real and important. Moreover, by doing something outrageous, they can set themselves apart so that at *least* they can recognize each *other* as real—for whatever that's worth.

Question: What about the other side of the coin, represented by the Ayn Rand—Nathaniel Branden philosophy of complete selfishness and their hatred of both Communism and all religions?

Campbell: As I pointed out before, you've got a real problem all your life selecting between the crackpots and the geniuses. You can take any idea and make it completely crackpot. For example:

Jesus' concept of Universal Brotherhood, the Prince of Peace: For years there were Christian armies crying, "Jesus, and no quarter!" And I repeat George Bernard Shaw's remark: "It seems to me Christianity is a great idea; too bad somebody doesn't try it."

Question: Assuming that we may have to get our number listed in some cosmic "telephone directory," will we go into space as a unified *Terran* culture or remain relatively autonomous—Russians, Americans, British, French, etc.?

Campbell: There are some people who can't tell one Chinese from another, and probably Chinese to whom all Caucasians look alike. If an Oriental or Caucasian can't differentiate between members of each race, what's a Sagittarian going to think of a human being? *They* won't be able to tell one of us from another—and *they* won't be interested in the slightest in our individual differences, except possibly to notice that we tend to be divided into roughly about two and a half different subgroups. They're going to assume that we're all alike, and we're going to be *treated* alike . . . with the interesting consequence that if you as a Terrestrian want to be reasonably treated by the Galactics, you had better see to it that your fellow Terrestrians damned well behave themselves. If they do *not*, the reaction of the Galactics will be pretty much the same to all Terrestrians. It'd better be some sort of Terran Police Force to impose "good behavior" (in Galactic terms) on all Terrans.

Question: You're on record as advocating the licensing of out-and-out quacks. Why?

Campbell: A quack is somebody who practices medicine in a manner not approved by the American Medical Association. By definition, this includes Louis Pasteur, Joseph Lister, Semmelweis, Jenner, and Harvey, who did *not* practice medicine in the orthodox concept of their time and place. They happened to be *right* and the authorities of the day were all wrong. Semmelweis, the man who solved the problem of childbed (puerperal) fever, faced the combined power of all the medical societies of Europe. They succeeded in driving him to his own death—as effective a job of squelching as you can imagine. What I'm saying is: we should license quacks. They are experimenting. There are some things that I feel are *ultimately* unethical in the behavior of the American Medical Association. I consider them immoral in this respect: they know for a fact that their prescribed methods of treatment for certain conditions have a 100 percent death rate—that their present methods of treatment—the best they know how—are *totally* incompetent. And yet they will not permit their patients to *try* some other method. They do everything in their power—by legal methods, by economic methods and so forth—to make it impossible for a patient to receive any other kind of treatment. If you *know* that you are incapable of curing this child of leukemia, do you have any ethical right to prevent his trying something else? *Anything* else? This, I object to very deeply. I consider it immoral. Yet this is what the AMA is doing.

Question: In one issue of Analog you wrote, "I am strongly in favor of rigidly segregated schools . . . that our schools be segregated considerably more rigidly than they are today." It sounds like a return to the sixteenth century. What are you advocating?

Campbell: I was having a little fun with my readers to make them stop quoting quotations and start *thinking*. I was, at that time, sending my daughter to a rigidly segregated school after having taken her out of the horribly *un*segregated public school. The school she went to was rigidly segregated; they didn't let morons in as first-class students. She had a Liberian girl as a roommate, a couple of Ghanese boys as classmates up there, but it was a segregated school because they didn't let the *dopes* in. Schools should be segregated and it must be acknowledged that not all human beings are equal; some people are smarter than others. They always have been and always will be. It's not a question of how much education they've got. It's a question of what their built-in individual potentials are. If you don't make your school appropriate to the potential of the individual, you're either trying to force him beyond his greatest capabilities, thus frustrating him and making him feel incompetent, or you are *not* giving him sufficient stimulation. The latter results in boredom and dropouts, the former often in social or self-destructive acts. The very intelligent student doesn't get sufficient stimulation. He'll be convinced: "Oh, it's all a lot of nonsense," and he'll drift away. You won't have an educated *man* there, either. *I want segregated schools*—segregated on the basis of abilities—and I do not want schools in which the distribution is by racial proportions. That has absolutely nothing whatever to do with it. If it turns out 90 percent Negro and only 10 percent White, that's just the way it's going to have to *be*. It makes no difference what the skin color is, what counts is how much brainpower the individual has. I think one of the *stupidest* school boycotts ever tried was the one here in New York where some Negroes were protesting the non-integration of the special schools in New York designed for the mentally retarded. *How* do you expect to integrate—on the basis of racial proportions—schools for the mentally retarded? That's *not* what they're for. They are for the maximum *possible* training of unfortunate individuals.

Question: In another editorial you state: "God is not democratic. He violates every basic tenet of Democracy. Naturally such a concept is intolerable in a democratic society." What do you mean by "God"?

Campbell: Well, the usual Christian concept of

God. When using a term, you either have to work with the general popular definition *or* define your term in the particular piece you're writing. In the usual concept, God is the Omnipotent, Omniscient Power. He is the King of Heaven. He determines what is Right and what is Wrong. All of these concepts are specifically *anti*-democratic. In a democracy, the proposition is that the Will of the People determines the truth. That is *false*. It has never worked and it never will. It won't work because man is *not* God. Man is not omnipotent and man is not all-wise. When he sets himself up as a sort of collective form of God, he's *not* God, he's nuts—just as nuts as anyone in the local insane asylum who announces that *he* is God! Humanity is *not* God. We don't know the answers—and if we fall for the delusion that we do, and lose the humility of being willing to learn, well, pride goeth before sudden death.

CHAPTER 10
Cosmic Cycles, Climate, and World Civilization

Eventually we must all come to terms with the reality of our personal mortality. In an abstract way I have always been intrigued with various cyclical rhythms of the human body and their relationship to the greater rhythms of the Earth, those of the planets and the Sun's still-mysterious "beats"—finally out to include the Galaxy and entire cosmos.

Our lives too are cycles with a beginning, a middle, and an end. The laws of thermodynamics state that all living things, the Earth itself, the Sun—even the Universe—will run down and reach energy point zero.

Everything has its cycle, short or long, small and large, and Edward B. Dewey, author of *Cycles: The Mysterious Forces that Trigger Events* (New York: Hawthorne, 1969), is the father of this new science. Through his lifelong study of cycles, thousands of which have been found in the natural sciences, medicine, economics, and political affairs, Dewey believes that man will eventually solve one of the deepest mysteries of the Universe: why events in Nature and in human affairs repeat themselves with such astounding regularity.

When that happens, the laws of physics as they are presently understood will have to be changed to include paraphysics and the study of the solar (as well as galactic and universal) *superspectrum*. It won't come as a surprise to discover that Superior Beings have evolved in many star systems—in a pluriverse of increasingly refined echelons of never-ending "nonphysical" dimensions.

That—or as close as we can come to it—will be the denouement.

We'll look at some surprising physical cycles here, that, as Dewey says, "puts us on the threshold of a completely different and extraordinary way of life for all mankind." It's true that biologists have long studied variations in animal populations over periods of time, economists have studied the ups and downs of business activity, and market analysts have studied fluctuations in the prices of common stocks. Our present understanding of cycles is about where physiology stood before Lavoisier showed that animal respiration is a slow combustion process.

When Chap Hiskins was managing editor of *Forbes* magazine, he told Dewey (then director of the University of Pittsburgh's Center for Interdisciplinary Cycle Research) that bank debits surged upward every three months. But it was when a man named Copley Amory sponsored an international biological conference that Dewey learned there were *regular* changes in the abundance of wildlife. This put him firmly and "irrevocably on the trail of the great cycle mystery."

And what a mystery it is.

Just for openers, he learned that peaks in the abundance of the Canadian lynx occur on the average of every 9.6 years; he studied the records of the Hudson's Bay Company from 1735 up to 1969 and discovered twenty-four peaks in the number of lynx skins at intervals averaging 9.6 years.

Atlantic fishermen have the most abundant catches every 9.6 years. Snowshoe rabbits in Canada, chinch bugs in Illinois, martens, fishers, owls, and hawks also have peak populations every 9.6 years. The incidence of heart disease in New England peaks every 9.6 years—as does the average harvest of wheat in the United States. But there are all kinds of other cycles as well. Hordes of Norway lemmings rush to the sea and drown themselves by the millions every 3.9 years! Why? Regular and predictable cycles have also been observed in grasshoppers, flies, gnats, nematodes, and hundreds of other insects.

What invisible, unidentified force regulates and balances the *trillions* of cycles (often within other cycles) of living things? What integrates them into the perfect harmony of the planetary biosphere? As we've seen, all the energy needed comes from the Sun, which has its own cycles, "beats," and fluctuations. The Earth-Moon system and all the planets with *their* satellites, electromagnetic and gravitational fields, are integrated with the one huge, everlasting, deep, bass solar "song" of life—its radiation, the solar wind and the *superspectrum*.

This is the Music of the Spheres sought by Copernicus and Kepler.

But for us, as human beings, there are also world cycles of civilization that rise and fall with cold-wet to cold-dry cycles, and warm-dry to warm-wet cycles. As we've seen before, a global drop in temperature of only a few degrees can cause a cataclysmic ice age, so these cold, warm, dry, wet periods are *extremely* important. Understanding something of the past helps us—even if only empirically—to know something of the future.

Dewey freely admits the speculative nature of his findings, but he is not blind to their implications: "We have overwhelming evidence that some kinds of environmental forces must exist that alternately stimulate and depress mankind in the mass. These same forces also affect plant life, animal life, even the weather. It would be statistically unreasonable to think they are the result of chance."

If there were indeed great cataclysms that threw the entire Earth in upheaval during remote historical epochs, there must also have been some havens of safety—in fact many places where the forces of Nature bypassed the environment, leaving it in peace and tranquility. One piece of supporting evidence may be the 17.3-year cycle observed in the thickness and thinness of the sedimentary deposits at the bottom of Crimea's Lake Saki that is present in each fifth of the series, or intervals of 86½ years, going back to 2295 B.C. The cycles in each segment are in exact step.

No matter how long the span of his data, Dewey's cycles stayed constant. There is an 11.2-year cycle in the index of international battles that had the same period before the death of Christ as it has now.

Yet the established sciences have decreed, for example, that Darwin's theory of evolution is the very last, most authoritative word about how life arose from a primordial ball of mud spinning around a coalescing protostar. Somehow, from this primitive unicellular slime came the millions of different shapes, forms, sizes, colors, and functions of all living things. Then from the apes (or the rats, depending on your bias), there arose an intelligent creature that developed consciousness, with a pattern-perceiving brain. With this brain, it probed and solved the secrets of its environment, then refined these studies into disciplines called sciences. Afterward, some of these creatures "imagined" they had been created by a Superior Being (or group of archangelic entities) "from the heavens."

But others, more intelligent, therefore more scientific, clearly perceived that mankind had arisen from chaos by pure chance—the result of a series of *stupendously* fortunate accidents of Nature.

We'll see.

Professor Paul Kurtz correlates the popularity of astrology with moral decay and the rise of Nazism in Germany in the early 1930s. The philosophy professor from the State University of New York at Buffalo feels that only a relentless and "merciless" attack on all forms of obscurantism by his Committee for the Scientific Investigation of Claims of the Paranormal is healthy for both science and society.

Professor Kurtz does not want to see the spirit of academic skepticism eroded. In this, he's completely in agreement with Charles Hoy Fort, whose main point was to teach young people to doubt just about everything they were told by scientific authorities. Of course, the fact that this includes the vigilantism of the Committee (well, let's call it CSICP, which seems as good an acronym as any) does chafe a bit but Kurtz is nothing if not sincerely determined to censor or exterminate all forms of "irrationalism" (except, perhaps, his own?). This includes astrology, Velikovskiism, UFOlogy, numerology, and a host of subjects defined by CSICP as "obscurantism," particularly belief in religions and/or faith in God.

"There is always the danger," said Kurtz, "that once irrationality grows, it will spill over into other areas. There is no guarantee that a society so infected by unreason will be resistant to even the most virulent programs of dangerous ideological sects." Many of his own colleagues have recoiled from his overkill.

It won't be long before the Committee trains its guns on biorhythm and decides that the study of cycles is also heresy. Before that happens, a closer look at the historical effect of cycles in weather might be something of an obstacle to the "humanist-materialist" schools which now teach evolution as the only explanation for life on this planet. Considering the fact that, at this writing, no one has ever—in the history of science—seen any living thing metamorphose into an entirely different genus or species, any more than any human being has—to my knowledge (this is apt to change at any moment)—observed life anywhere else within the solar system, it would seem that evolution, à la Darwin, is a bit too strong a stand considering the evidence. In actual practice it is *dogma*.

Today stress is blamed for everything from headaches and ulcers to alcoholism and nervous breakdowns. On the other hand, according to Dr. Robert Sharpe, a behavior therapist for the London University Health Service, "*under*stress can cause depression, indigestion, alcoholism, overeating, tension, fatigue and headaches. It is impossible to determine the exact number of people suffering from understress," he says, but according to the general breakdown of modern society, it could affect distinctly different classes of people.

"Understress can actually result in loss of incentive to live, inability to concentrate, loss of confidence, careless, slow thinking, and chronic irritability," Dr. Sharpe emphasized.

In line with this, the long historical cycles of famine, extreme cold, and other hardships causing human misery that have followed periods of prosperity and warmth may be Nature's intentional way of stirring up the "broth" of the biosphere, thereby creating stress and keeping life from stagnating.

The effect of climate on man was studied by Dr. Raymond H. Wheeler, former Chief of Staff of the Climate Division of the Weather Science Foundation in Illinois. As an expert political scientist whose main work was in the field of psychology, he dealt with experimental, educational systematic, and Gestalt psychology, the psychology of the blind, and with climate, history, and human behavior.

While at the University of Kansas, Professor Wheeler plunged into an immense project summarizing all of recorded history in an organized fashion. "Where there are many climates," he said to *Business Week* magazine in 1950, "there will be many forms of men . . . and for every geographic locality there is an answering type of humanity. This is the explanation of the energy of human life and the development of civilizations.

"Since the time of ancient Greece and Egypt, scientists have recorded their judgment that man, in profound and sundry ways, is affected by the climatic characteristics of his environment. In cooler climates man is more vigorous, more aggressive, more persistent, stronger physically, larger, braver in battle, healthier, and less prone to sexual overindulgence. In warm climates man is more timid, smaller, physically weaker and less courageous, but more inclined to physical pleasures, more effeminate, lazier, and less aggressive."

In order to test the results of his research, Professor Raymond Wheeler experimented with rats to learn how they would behave under widely varying temperatures. He raised one group of rats at 90° F., another at 55°. The rats had to work their way through a maze to find food. The rats raised in cold learned the path four times as fast as the "hot" rats, and were bigger, more alert, healthier, and more independent. The cold-weather females built neat nests and took excellent care of their young. But the hot-weather female rats not only did *not* build nests, they sometimes ate their young. They lacked energy and aggressiveness, the two main qualities humans must have to protect their rights.

Wheeler drew up a rough pattern of how human beings had behaved for nearly 3,000 years, and then in 1935, he projected his orderly weather curve into the future—with a list of predictions of what would happen during the fifteen years until 1950. Professor Wheeler predicted a "war season" in the late 1930s. His prophesy was fulfilled by the rise of Hitler. He foresaw another set of events after 1944, which was toward the end of the long hot phase that had brought two world wars.

He said that as the world cooled there would be a democratic revival.

Although it does generally seem that the northernmost nations (in the northern hemisphere) win every war against their southern neighbors, in and of themselves, Wheeler's theories would probably find many detractors today. Yet Jean Bodin, a famous political writer in the sixteenth century, came to the same conclusions, as did the English physician Richard Mead in his *Treatise Concerning the Influence of the Sun and Moon upon Human Bodies*. When John Arbuthnot wrote his *Essay Concerning the Effect of Air on Human Bodies*, he observed that despotism was more frequent in the south and democracy farther advanced in the north. "Governments are powerless to change the genius and temper of a race against the force of air and climate," he claimed.

Professor Wheeler echoed Arbuthnot: "Peoples of cooler climates treasured liberty, were averse to slavery, built democratic societies. Warmer climates, it was noticed, were conducive to the more reflective pursuits; the birth rate was much higher in the colder regions though there were more women, proportionately, in the warm countries, and the warmer races were considered to be emotionally less stable and dependable."

In the sixteenth century, Jean Bodin observed that "The northern races were more faithful to their governments but less fanatic in religion and they were more tolerant, docile, and gayer, more trustworthy and less cunning." The southern and warmer races, said Bodin, were "more melancholic, malicious, foxy, cruel, less democratic, and more given over to slaves, tyrants, and dictators. Aristotle commented on the willingness of people in the south to remain in subjection."

From Montesquieu, who made much the same observations in his *Spirit of the Laws* in 1748, to Professor Ellsworth Huntington, Yale University's geographer and climatologist, who reached the same conclusions in *The Mainsprings of Civilization* (New York: John Wiley & Sons, 1951), all recorders seem in agreement.

Dr. A. E. Douglass, the Lowell Observatory astronomer at Flagstaff, Arizona, who studied rings on 1,500-year-old Arizona yellow pines, observed that during some years the rings were fat, in other years scrawny. The thickness, he suggested, was caused by moisture and the leanness by drought. Thus the trees had "written" in their rings a 1,500-year weather diary. Douglass checked his idea against more than a century of reliable weather records and found it stood up perfectly.

He then studied more than one million rings, and when he charted the results, discovered a rhythm to the weather curve—with hot and cold, wet and dry periods alternating at regular intervals. Moreover, his curve was virtually identical to Professor Wheeler's cultural curve.

Was there a *world* pattern? With the help of as many as forty assistants at a time, Dr. Douglass searched for indirect evidence to trace world climatic changes by studying tree rings on California's giant sequoias, which were more than 3,000 years old. The correlation was visible almost from the beginning. Scrawny sequoia rings reflected severe drought in California in the 1290s B.C. At the same time there was plague and famine in Egypt and droughts and crop failures in China and India. Thus, according to the evidence of the tree rings, the biblical plagues and famines would have occurred, just as Velikovsky had deduced, during hot, dry times.

World weather fell into a pattern, repeated in orderly fashion. The researchers found a giant 1,020-year cycle, within which were three smaller cycles of 510 years, 170 years, and 100 years. Human behavior at various points on the curve revealed immediate evidence that there was one pattern of behavior for warm periods and another for cold. People behaved rather badly during long periods of warmth and entirely differently during cold periods.

Warm periods were marked by tyranny, dictatorship, international wars, and various other excesses. Great military leaders showed up with unerring regularity during the hot periods—Attila the Hun, William the Conqueror, Charlemagne, Napoleon, Hitler, Rommel, Eisenhower, and MacArthur. According to J. D. Ratcliff in *Nation's Business*, "Ninety percent of all Jewish persecutions occurred in warm periods."

It was during warm times that Christians were thrown to the lions in Rome. Beginning in 585 B.C. with Nebuchadnezzar's war on Jerusalem up to Napoleon and then Hitler, despotism and wars occurred with 90 percent accuracy in hot periods.

Cold phases—when the world thermometer

dropped, sometimes not more than a couple of degrees—produced a different pattern of events. People became more aggressive and independent. The yoke of oppression was thrown off. The American and French Revolutions took place during a cold period. The same democratic surge manifested itself throughout the world at the same time. There were revolts or civil wars in Mexico, Turkey, India, Siam, and Belgium.

The great social reforms came about during cold periods. Ninety-two percent of the kings and leaders whom history proclaimed as "great" lived during cold periods, among them, Jesus Christ, the Emperor Constantine, Charles Martel, Luther, Calvin, Washington, and Lincoln.

Adam Ferguson, obviously influenced by Montesquieu, stressed in his *History of Civil Society* that a temperate climate was best for mankind "for it produces superior traits. The answer is to be found in the effects of climate on human physiology."

Two twentieth-century economists Henry L. Moore and Edgar Lawrence Smith, authors of *Tides in the Affairs of Men* (New York: Macmillan, 1939), indicated that economic and production cycles are closely related to climatic changes. Smith believes there is an economic response to solar changes. "Within the economic pattern of a period, the tidal ebb and flow of mass psychology in response to the rhythms of cosmic environmental change cannot be disregarded."

The Russian investigator, A. L. Tchijewski, author of *Cosmic Energy as a Factor in Human History*, a paper published in 1949, found a direct relationship between wars and the sunspot cycle, and firmly believes in the effect of ionization of the atmosphere on man's activities.

A study of changes in human thought and attitude over a ten-year period was discovered almost by accident, and was at first confined to changes in viewpoints in the histories of psychology, biology, and philosophy. It seemed almost impossible that all through history these three subjects fluctuated in rhythms from one viewpoint to its opposite and back again *by chance alone*.

It became downright mystifying when researchers discovered that other sciences were changing in precisely the same way, *and in sync!* "Fashions in science," said a mathematical physicist named Schroedinger in the early 1950s, "seem to be strangely synchronized." The "coincidence" demanded further studies into literature, art, music—even political history.

"The same pattern has repeated in so many ways," said Dr. W. F. Peterson in his four-volume work on *The Patient and the Weather*, "in so many countries and cultures, in so amazingly a precise and objective manner, that the results seemed almost uncanny. A rough curve was drawn of these seesaw movements, actions and reactions, characteristic of entire culture-patterns, north and south, east and west, covering every known country in the world upon which historical information could be obtained. Then another amazing incident happened..."

When he investigated the sequoia tree-ring curves of Dr. A. E. Douglass and Ellsworth Huntington, Peterson instantly recognized the parallels between the culture curve and the tree curves. The peaks and valleys found in the culture curve corresponded with the tree growth curve in a way that chance alone could not possibly explain. The tree-ring curve immediately suggested a climatic explanation for the cultural curve, and vice-versa. When all the possible information about the history of climate was assembled, lo and behold, the data truly warranted the correlation of alternating cold and warm, wet and dry periods of history with changes in fashion, style, warfare, peace, art and commerce—the whole kit and kaboodle!

"What lies beyond 1950?" asked author J. T. Ratcliff, in "The Weather Tells Our Future," in the March, 1950, issue of *Nation's Business* magazine,

"The rest of this century will be generally cold, with the thermometer climbing to the warm side for two short periods, in 1952 and 1970. Since war occurs almost solely in warm weather periods, these are danger points [*Korea and Vietnam?*] If we get over these bumps we should have peace until the year 2000 when the world will start warming up again. . . .

"We will go back to the cold weather pattern that ruled the Victorian era. The last half of the nineteenth century was generally cold. The last half of the twentieth will be similarly cold. *Our tastes will change to conform to the Victorian pattern.*"

Greater stress will develop for individuals during the cold period, but there will be other, more profound changes. Rather than submerging himself, the solid individual will seek greater self-expression. "In the hot twenties and thirties all men strove to dress alike," said Raymond H. Wheeler. "In the cooler sixties and seventies, there will be forerunners of much brighter male plumage." As far as weather is concerned, Wheeler's theory covered the anomalous climatology of the late 1970s almost perfectly, so it would appear that we are dealing with something more than a hare-brained theory. We seem to have *another* new science on our hands. Perhaps it may be called "Psychoclimatology." (After all, who would have believed, only twenty-five years ago, that there would soon be someone called a "biological engineer?")

"Just as governments tend to centralize in warm periods, so do people," Wheeler said. "They flock to the cities. When cold weather arrives, this is reversed. A back-to-the-country movement is already underway and will continue to grow." He predicts less divorce during the final decades of the twentieth century, stricter morals, better manners, and greater happiness. At the same time there will be a resurgence of democratic principles even in totalitarian nations.

Economically, Wheeler notes that business depressions always occur in dry periods. "A religious revival always occurs in cold periods—the mystical, intellectual concept of God giving way to the personal God of the evangelical religions."

In the long run, Wheeler foresees a tremendous crisis arising in 1999, one that will engulf the world in the year 2000, "at which point the 510- and 170-year cycles come together." (Rome's final collapse came when the two curves met, and Charlemagne's empire fell apart. At another point of convergence, the Middle Ages gave way to the Renaissance. In each instance, an old world died and a new one was born.)

Other prophesies also forecast similar events. What will the new world which will be born in the year 2000 look like? Wheeler believes it will be a Super Renaissance, far broader, more dramatic, and intense than the one that occured in the fifteenth century.

"The new world will not be governed by Communism, but by a new democracy broader and more effective than any the world has known to date."

In 1965, four years after I received a copy of the interpretation of the Hindu Kali Yuga World Cycle from 1912 to 2010, divided into seven-year subcycles, I published it in *Astrology: The Space-Age Science* (New York: New American Library, 1968). This was given to Nora Forrest, a well-known mundane or "state" astrologer, in 1946 in Pittsburgh by a blind man named McDermott, who, according to astro-meteorologist George J. McCormack, had received it from "an Indian national" some time after World War I.

Without covering it in its entirety, it is interesting to note that the Cold War was predicted for the 1954-1961 period, along with a coalition of the Nordic and western European nations into a possible United States of Europe.

The 1961-1968 period (Sun/positive) predicted the greatest of all the Catholic popes and the election of America's first Catholic President. "Asia and Africa may be unfriendly to the United States."

For 1968-1975 (Moon/positive) economic hardships, reforms in taxation. "Racially, the Arab peoples will be feeling the strength of unity and it will take statesmanship to keep the new power within bounds."*

1975-1982 (Mars/negative) Rumors of wars and dissatisfaction with world-governing body's restraints on nations are indicated. Possible war will threaten from Arabs and from eastern Asia. Since this is a negative Mars cycle, the period of peace will not end entirely. This is the time in which natural cataclysms will take place. Disunity in the Balkans and restlessness in Central Europe and Africa are still problems in the world.

1982-1989 (Uranus/positive) The 1920s negative Uranus cycle popularizes the subconscious mind. This period will bring forth a science of superconsciousness. This is a wonderful time for a new superpsychology, the spread of occult wisdom and vast voyages into worlds hitherto unknown. The United States and Russia dominate the world and their policies may still be at cross purposes that will end in disaster. This will be a period of great explosion in many ways.

1989-1996 (Jupiter/negative) This is very bad for organized religion. Jupiterian optimism and belief in goodness and peace may lead to blindness about troublesome things people do not want to see or believe. During the second half of this cycle comes the Third Woe, with worldwide calamities.

1996-2003 (Saturn/positive) (Some scholars have placed the date of the beginning of the millennium here. But it seems unlikely this would occur in a Saturn cycle.) Yet, the great war ends in this period. The Jews will be the most fortunate people of the time.

2003-2010 (Neptune/negative) Time of the "Thousand Years of Peace" is indicated. If an ephemeris for those years were available today, astrologers could find the time for the beginning of the millennium and the Aquarian Age. It would certainly have to be a powerful and most benign configuration to justify the optimistic prophecies of the past 5,000 years of darkness.

According to the very ancient Chinese *Book of Odes,* an anthology of time-honored philosophy, mysticism, and metaphysical conclusions which furnished Confucius and the writers of the *Tao Te Ching* with the basic necessities for their teachings and poems, the world was once as it is now.

The cyclic nature of civilizations is also reflected in the sacred writings of the Egyptians, Persians, and Indians. The remnants of knowledge so painstakingly pieced together from all parts of the world by scholars such as Velikovsky, Ignatius Donnelly, and scores of more obscure workers suggest that the Hindu Yugas (there were four) or World Ages are cyclic records, or warnings, that what has happened in the forgotten past will, unless we guard against it, happen again—*perhaps by our own hands.*

The ancient Chinese encyclopedia, *Sing-li-tatsiuen-Chou,* recorded many destructions of mankind that ended each World Age. An ancient Greek writer named Hesiod told of five previous World Ages and the destruction of each. Whole generations perished before the repopulated planet could resume its interrupted cycles of history.

Ancient Hindu writers casually referred to devices that could only be machines that rolled on land or flew through the air. The Greeks clearly understood the atomic structure of matter. In his work, *On the Eternity of the World,* Philo of Alexandria tried to explain why the exact knowledge of great technological civilizations did not survive the ages: "By reason of the constant and *repeated* destructions of water and fire, later generations did not receive from the former the memory of the order and sequence of events."

C. E. Brasseur de Bourbourg, in his *History of the Civilized Nations of Mexico,* wrote: "Man had been created and life manifested four times." The Sibylline Oracles, which are now classified by both Jewish and Christian authorities as *"pseudepographa,"* predict that *two* World Ages are yet to come. After each great catastrophe (or Sun Age), the Earth shifts its axis and the Sun appears to change its course through the sky.

Trying to determine whether the separation of World Ages is a result of natural catastrophe or manmade disaster (or a combination of both) is a maddening dilemma for serious scholars. But the remarkable Philo presented a perfectly clear statement proving that he understood the concept of atomic accident: "Democrates and Epicurus postulate many World Ages," he wrote, "the origin of which they ascribe to mutual impacts and interlacing of atoms, and their destruction to the counterblows and collisions by the bodies so formed."

Are these world cycles inevitable? Can it be that the solar *superspectrum* triggers great man-made *and* natural changes at the same times? The Greek mathematician Heraclitus taught that all civilization ends in fire every 10,800 years. But Aristarchus of Samos taught that the Earth is destroyed twice every 2,484 years; once by fire, once by water.

These cycles of varying frequencies correspond to the L-field of the Earth and the many still unknown "beats" of the sun. How these could have been deduced by people of ancient times remains a mystery. A Greek historian, writing about Hipparchus, the ancient scientist and philosopher, said, "The Assyrians have not only preserved the memorials of seven and twenty myriads of years (270,000 years) as Hipparchus says they have, but likewise of whole apocatastases and periods of the Seven Rulers of the World."

In his first book, Cicero said that the Chaldeans had records of the stars for more than 370,000 years. Diodorus Siculus claims that their observations of the Universe spanned the tremendous period of 473,000 years! This is certainly a far cry from the Judaic-Christian period of less than 6,000 years.

And yet those great thinkers and scientists of the distant past knew of even longer periods of ancient knowledge. In 1914, Thomas Taylor, in his *Notes on Julius Firmicus Maternus* (Thorndyke), said: "Epigenes, Berosus, and Critodemes set the duration of astronomical observations by the Babylonians at from 490,000 to 720,000 years."

CHAPTER 11
The Seven Faces of God

The most astounding thing about our Universe is that there is something rather than nothing. Why does it exist? What is the "shape" of the Universe, and of space? How were the planets formed? What really goes on in the Sun? Why does what happens in Nature happen? Is it all just chance and chaos, or is it an expression of natural—or perhaps divine—law?

As one of the characters in a Mark Twain story observed, after a visit by the local clergyman, "The more he counted his virtues the faster we counted our silverware." That about sums it up. Surely, really "intelligent" people do not believe in some mythical God.

Yet some do. In any culture that lasts more than two generations and establishes some kind of generally recognized and approved set of rules dealing with the relationship of the sexes and some viable sort of economic system, the notion persists. Every known culture has had its religious institutions, very often with similar myths and legends of great Beings with superhuman powers. Indonesian mythology abounds in stories of good and evil, of men and giants, and the exotic, ineradicable notion that all religions are somehow based on the essential awareness of the divine in Nature.

The pantheism of the Asian and Polynesian peoples often reflects facets of each other's faiths. This is also true of Hindus, Hebrews, Buddhists, Mohammedans, and Christians, a condition that presents some interesting problems in all God-man relationships. Brahma, Krishna, and Siva (the Creator, Preserver, and Destroyer) are reflected in the Trinity of Christianity—Father, Son, and Holy Ghost.

Any attempt to answer the question, "Is existence merely the result of chance, and consciousness just an accident of blind evolutionary chaos," usually results in a reaffirmation of one's original bias. Nature seems to have decreed a balance in the number of girls born as compared to male births, some sort of pattern in the number of twins, as related to triplets—and triplets as related to the number of quadruplets. It may be that there are intangible laws governing the number of religious fanatics balanced against the number of atheists with a large sprinkling of agnostics and knee-jerk church-goers in between, depending on the needs of the times.

We know so little. Virtually nothing. *The Encyclopedia of Ignorance*, published early in 1978 by Pergamon Press, contains an incomplete compendium of what man does *not* know in the sciences—how gravity works, for instance, what force enables plants to produce flowers, and why we become addicted to drugs and alcohol. The book begins with an essay by Otto Frisch, who in the late 1930s coined the term "nuclear fission" and helped explain the phenomenon. He asks perhaps the biggest question of all: "Why?"

It's a refreshing change to be able to read experts setting forth the profundity of their ignorance rather than the profundity of their knowledge. Although scientists strive for "complete" theories, the most successful theories in physics are those that explicitly leave room for the unknown.

"Our ignorance of developmental biology," wrote Nobel laureate Francis H. C. Crick, who helped describe the double-helix shape of the genetic material DNA, "has the following curious feature. We understand how an organism can build molecules although the largest of them is far too minute for us to see, even with a high-powered microscope. Yet we do not understand how it builds a flower or a hand or an eye, all of which are plainly visible to us."

The most baffling and challenging void in this field

brings Dr. Crick suspensefully close to rediscovering the biodynamic L-field. All it would require is one transcendental glimpse to put the *overall* or surrounding nature of the L-field into proper focus. Instead, he ponders how a nervous system is constructed in an animal, how the nerves' growth is directed, and how nerves are hooked up to the brain.

In my estimation, the one imponderable is that any researcher can find as many staunch opinions on any subject as there are people who voice them. Some of us are bibical fundamentalists; but even here, there are many ways of interpreting Christianity and almost as many interpretations of Judaism. The One God Allah's spokesman is Muhammad. The One God Jehovah's spokesman is Jesus. Is one true and one false? Or are *both* true *and* false? Islands of sensitive Christian minorities tend to move with respectful caution in the plural seas of Islam. Groups of sensitive Jews had the same tendencies among huge Christian majorities. Yet throughout history men have slaughtered each other in the name of one god or another.

So what then is religion, and why do we need it? Toynbee defines it as "a human being's total concern for Man's World." Although godless and religionless cultures are *theoretically* possible, they are so extremely unlikely that it almost seems as though such a condition is against natural law. If so, then the "instrument" of this law—in this case the only physical energy system within effective proximity—would be the Sun. It's equally unlikely that man will free himself from total solar dependence for a long time to come (the anarchist Godwin once made the proclamation "Man is not free so long as there is a God"). Man has tended to create an Olympus or Paradise or Valhalla and people it with creatures who, while they were magnified and idealized, were primarily drawn from everyday life.

In *The Phenomenon of God*, Harvey Wheeler claims that "the attributes of these gods provided their creators with standards of behavior and achievement. Divine attributes were then collated and systematized into codes of ethics. These ultimately yielded up philosophy and science." On the other hand, it is difficult to imagine a more human, petty, jealous, vindictive, or wrathful God than the biblical Yahweh, or Jehovah.

The ethos of Islam is its attitude toward God; to his will Moslems submit; him they constantly praise and glorify; and in him alone they hope. He is awful, transcendent, almighty, just, loving, merciful, and good. No creature may be compared to him, and to him alone do Moslems pray.

The concept of Genesis, the origin of man, Sun worship, the solar *superspectrum*, and the idea of God have been pondered by many of the greatest thinkers of the past. Now it is time for man to use scientific knowledge in the search for his origins.

Several of the Polynesian sacred traditions refer to seven great nonphysical Beings which created the Sun, the planets, and then either *brought* man here or created all life, including mankind. According to Judeo-Christian tradition, the seven Elohim created the Universe (Job 1:6). The names of these great archangelic Beings are Ildaboath, Jehovah (Yahweh or Joa), Sabaoth, Adonai, Eloeus, Oreus, and Astanpheus. Elohim is the plural form, and of unknown origin.

According to Revelations (1:4, 5:6, 1:20), there were seven antithetical Beings or "rebellious angels" who rose up against the central figure, Yahweh, and made war in heaven.

The almost universal doctrine of creation functioned in a negative way by preventing an "idolatrous worship of nature" among certain ancient groups. It reminded them that although God is unchangeable, incorruptible, and all-sufficient, Nature is none of these things. Evil, therefore, is not possible for God but is possible for Nature, and is an *actuality* for man, who is able only intermittently and dimly to perceive the world *as* God's world, to discern the creator's splendor in his works.

To the Jews, the central figure of the Elohim was ineffable, his name unspeakable, sacred, and referred to only indirectly as YHWH. Yet the Elohim, or circle of heavenly Beings, *in their dialogue*, used the pronoun "our," and said, "let us" make him into our image and likeness.

Who or what, then *is* God?

Zoroastrianism, a later version of the ancient religion of Persia, called Mazdaism, has features almost identically congruent with Polynesian, Judaic, and Icelandic sacred legends. In each, there were seven great nonphysical Beings, the central entity became the God of one group's awareness and that tribe became "chosen" by the Creator. In Mazdaism, the Amesha Spentas reflected the Elohim of Judaism. The central figure was Ahura Mazda (also called Ormazd or Ormuzd), meaning Sovereign Knowledge. The lesser deities: Vohu Manah (Good Thought), Asha Vahista (Highest Righteousness), Khshathra Vairya (Divine Kingdom), Spenta Armaiti (Pious Devotion), Haurvatat (Salvation), and Ameretat (Immortality).

The seven negative entities (devils) or evil spirits were, curiously enough, called *daevas* or *divs*; their leader was Ahriman (or Angra Mainyu), probably the proto-figure of the Judaic, Christian, and Islamic Satan, ruler of the kingdom of darkness. In the struggle between Ahriman and Ahura Mazda, a Saviour, whose name is Saoshyant, will appear in the fourth period of the Universe. The ultimate triumph will be that of Ahura Mazda, who is represented in the form of the pure natural substances which he has created, *notably fire.*

The special veneration shown to fire, especially in the purification ritual of its religious ceremonies, once led to the erroneous belief that Zoroastrians were fire worshippers. The pre-Zoroastrian Magi acquired great power through some form of occult scientific prowess, which was demonstrated during elaborate purification rituals. According to legend, the Magi were Sun-worshippers, able to levitate people and inanimate objects. Scores of historical reports of levitation by serious chroniclers make the possibility of antigravity having been used in ancient times worthy of careful consideration.

Robert Charroux, in *One Hundred Thousand Years of Man's Unknown History* (Paris: 1961), gives scores of documented reports of levitation—"The enormous blocks of stone, weighing as much as six hundred tons . . . have been transported by levitation and put into place with extreme ease.

"What the ancients actually knew about those forces and how they used electricity and magnetism to overcome gravity is almost impossible to determine, because of the religious mystery that surrounded the initiates' operations."

With notably few exceptions, such as Nikola Tesla and lesser known inventors who have "done the impossible," levitation, especially in Europe, diminished as experimental science developed. There seem to be two or more entirely different avenues of knowledge and power—avenues that, at certain times and under certain conditions, may cross or run parallel for a brief time. One of these is the presently known path of the physical sciences. For lack of a better term, the other would appear to be sheer magic, given our present understanding.

All the evidence indicates that Tesla was undoubtedly on the right track when he told his admirers that invisible worlds, with intelligent Beings, could exist among us, side by side, without our knowledge or awareness. Such worlds, or dimensions, just as "real" to their inhabitants as ours is to us, would exist on an entirely different vibrational plane. If so, then by changing the frequency of our perception to several trillion more vibrations per second, it might be possible to see the world, the Sun, the entire Universe in a way that is inconceivable to the human brain in its present state.

The farther we move from three-dimensional science the closer we come to the worlds of science fiction, fantasy, magic—and religion. There are entirely too many parallels among all the great faiths for them *not* to have had a common origin. The Pentateuch, or five books of Moses, has a parallel in the Zend Avesta, or five books of Zoroastrianism: the

Avesta, the *Yasna*, the *Gathas*, the *Yashts*, and the *Videvdat* (a code of purity virtually identical to Leviticus).

In modified form, Mazdaism survives among the Parsis in India, the Ghebers in Iran, the Jews (particularly during the time of the Captivity), the Gnostics and even Manichaeans. The Zoroastrian Saviour, the Hebrew Messiah, the Islamic Prophet, and Christian Redeemer are all essentially the same concept. A common thread of "illumination" is manifest in the lives of the prophets Moses, Jesus, Mohammad, and their Indian counterpart, Siddhartha Gautama (Buddha—"the enlightened one"). Despite the chronological disparity, each holy man seems to reflect the transcendental experience of Zoroaster. There were many others, including the Persian Mani, who was banished by Shapur I (at the behest of the Zoroastrian priests), exiled for twenty years, and then beaten to death on the orders of Bahram I in 275 A.D. for daring to call himself the Paraclete and successor to Zoroaster, Buddha, and Jesus.

We seem to create "suitable" mental compartments among nondisparate concepts. There is a tendency, at the extreme limits of scientific awareness and knowledge, to perceive something very real but ineffable and somehow almost insubstantial. Particle physicists and astronomers, for example, often give rather odd reports of experiences and their reactions at the borderline of the known. The search for the "ultimate" particle has produced names such as "strange," "psi," and even "charm" to describe the particle's characteristics.

There are many scientists, like Tesla, who achieve incredible "breakthroughs" that they would not report—formally or informally—particularly to their colleagues, because they know the terrible effects of ridicule and the pain of ostracism—even exile. You can't help suspect, however, that scientists with the courage to talk freely about their experiences (and *feelings*, which could not exist unless the Laws of the Universe permitted or *desired* them) would find many others eager to do the same.

Albert Einstein who, thanks to the aberration of the Nazi uprising, fled to the United States, was very uneasy about Heisenberg's "uncertainty principle"—which, in essence, said that nothing in the Universe is predictable because everything is constantly changing. "I cannot believe," said the pacifist/violinist/mathematician, "that God plays dice with the Universe."

As good as his word, Einstein redoubled his efforts in the search for a unifed theory that would apply to the infinitesimally small as well as the cosmic, in the hope that he could reinstate a logos for all of Nature.

In conformance with the yin-yang principle, there are often wholly materialistic (almost nihilistic) points of view about the supreme creator. Michael Novak (Harvard, Stanford, New York University), author of *Belief and Unbelief*, believes that according to the world's great creation myths "gods ordinarily arise out of nothingness." Scientists who share this viewpoint have stated that the myth credits the gods with too much power: "other factors like invasions, faminies, plagues, migration, and just plain chance also worked alongside gods to produce change. Old Testament thunder-gods are fine for nomads, but they won't do for farmers; legalistic bookkeeping gods are fine for tradesmen, but not for what Charles Reich calls Consciousness III."

"I assume," said Charles Wheeler, "that cultures of the future will continue to be characterized by very high rates of change and consequently that their religions will have to exhibit some integration of utopian and conservative ingredients into the same system. The major task will be to create a new and more compelling heavenly city, for it is the utopian component—and dynamism—that is lacking in today's belief systems. Science, economics, and politics now claim they can provide us with everything promised by St. Augustine's God, and more besides—a land of peace and freedom rather than one of milk and honey, a Camelot rather than a Green Pastures myth."

A far broader view might indicate that just as there are weather cycles of warm and cold, there are alternating cycles of science and magic, and that they sometimes overlap. We seem to be coming full cycle once again.

There is a very ancient Indian chronicle called the *Book of Dzyan*, a most remarkable collection of reports and legends pre-dating biblical history as we know it. Several thousand years ago, ancient scholars put into manuscript form tales of incredible happenings. Until the past few decades, few scientists would have given more than a passing glance to a story relating that scores of thousands of years ago a large metal ship came to the Earth and circled the planet several times before landing.

The Beings who emerged from the spaceship *"lived to themselves and were revered by the humans among whom they settled. But eventually differences arose among them and they divided their numbers, several of the men and women and some children settling in another city where they were promptly installed as rulers by the awe-stricken populace. But separation did not bring peace to these people, and finally their anger reached a point where the ruler of the original city took with him a small number of his warriors and they rose into the air in a huge shining metal vessel.*

"While they were still many leagues from the city of their enemies, they launched a great shining lance that rode on a beam of light. It burst apart in the city of their enemies with a great ball of flame that shot up to the heavens almost to the stars. All those in the city were horribly burned and even those who were not in the city—but nearby—were burned also. Those who looked upon the lance and the ball of fire were blinded forever afterward. Those who entered the city on foot became ill and died. Even the dust of the city was poisoned as were the rivers that flowed through it. Men dared not go near it, and gradually it crumbled into dust and was forgotten by men.

"When the leader saw what he had done to his own people, he retired to his palace and refused to see anyone. Then he gathered around him those of his warriors who remained and their wives and their children, and they entered into their vessels and rose one by one into the sky and sailed away. Nor did they return."

Judging from what we know today, the lance may have been a rocket with a nuclear warhead—guided by a laser beam. The ball of flame—could it have been a nuclear fireball? Was the atmosphere *poisoned* by radioactivity?

Tales of mysterious visitors from distant stars, perhaps from other galaxies, have existed in the legends, ballads, and written chronicles of every civilization that has inhabited our Earth. Dr. Morris K. Jessup, astronomer, astrophysicist, mathematician, and archaeologist, devoted years to excavating the ruins of great civilizations in Central America. The enormous stonework, he said, "is the result of the use of the power of levitation—by spaceships from other worlds—in antediluvian times.

"All centers of civilization and cultural renaissance recognized by present-day anthropologists," he added, "are but the surviving remnants of an empire and civilization which colonized the world a hundred thousand years ago."

Despite a few addlepated detractors who prefer to believe *he* was a crackpot because he committed suicide in 1959, Dr. Jessup was, in fact, a solid scientist whose research resulted in several thousand new discoveries of physical double-stars now catalogued in the *Memoirs of the Royal Astronomical Society* in London. He was engaged by the Carnegie Institution in Washington to investigate the Inca ruins of Peru. He received his doctorate in astrophysics at the University of Michigan and constructed and operated the largest refracting telescope in the southern hemisphere in South Africa. He also investigated the sources of crude rubber in the headwaters of the Amazon for the U.S. Department of Agriculture.

"Throughout the world," said Dr. Jessup, "civilization everywhere seems to have borrowed from a single antediluvian, vastly advanced *proto-culture*." This planet has probably seen wave after wave of cultural implantation. Legends everywhere indicate that women on the Earth have mated with aliens from the stars—and have borne their children.

"Mechanical flight," Dr. Jessup once wrote, "has been established by written records at a remote time of maybe 70,000 to 200,000 years ago."

The fantastic stone masonry found all over the world was not developed in the same way modern engineers would go about it. The old "rope and pulley, block and tackle" explanations, in which slaves are supposed to have lifted 50- and 100-ton blocks of granite hundreds of feet into the air is obviously ridiculous.

Yet the incredibly ancient site of Sacsahuaman gives every indication of having been a great resort on a high mountaintop overlooking what is now the modern Peruvian city of Cuzco. The lower three tiers are very heavy, hard, dark basalt. The smallest blocks of stone in these walls weigh several hundred pounds; some of the larger ones are exactly twelve feet square at the base and rise to a height of eighteen to twenty feet. The average stones weigh well over 200 tons each and could easily crush some of our heaviest earth-moving machinery.

"All of them," according to Dr. Jessup, "were crudely rough-quarried, and were then ground into their designated niches in the structure by pushing them back and forth *in situ* until they fitted so closely, completely, and accurately that even today a knife blade cannot be inserted between them. This is a logical and practical shortcut to effective stone fitting which we have not equalled in modern engineering.

"These antediluvians possessed a form of raw power; they controlled an elemental force which enabled them to construct edifices to astound and startle later generations of Terrestrials. Evidence shows that *something* interrupted the construction of most of these ancient buildings; almost universally, the original builders disappeared and left no trace whatever of their real identity."

The ruins of Baalbeck are among the oldest, most mysterious, and majestic artifacts on Earth. The great city is currently believed to have been devoted to the worship of Baal or Bel, allegedly the Sun-god of that antediluvian period. The struggle between the polytheistic Canaanites and the worship of the God of Israel combined ethical, political, and national elements. The final detestation of the name Baal by the Hebrews is seen in the use of the name Beelzebub, which is probably the same as Baalzebub . . . which is the same as Satan. So those who are believed to have worshipped the Sun were considered identical to devil worshippers. A rather mysterious coincidence, it's hard to believe that the builders of what is now called Baalbeck were ignorant. Perhaps instead of worshipping the Sun, these masters of levitation were somehow attuned to the solar *superspectrum*.

Who were they? There isn't a shred of evidence to show when or by whom—or even how—this colossal structure was built. It was there thousands of years before the ancient nomadic Semites drove their camels across the desert sands. Its design is sheer grandeur, its execution the epitome of grace. Nothing built during the past thirty centuries in that part of the world can equal it. Was there a connection between these architect/levitators and very advanced nonhuman Beings?

What about genesis? *Was* man created by God? Did humankind arise from the primordial slime with all other life forms, or are we the descendants of space-faring superhuman Beings?

Possibly—*anything*. But the predominating legend of the seven great spiritual Beings strikes too resounding a chord. We may never discover the true identity of the Amesha Spentas (or the Elohim), but insofar as it is possible to speculate, the concept of a vastly advanced race of Superior Beings is not too far removed from present scientific theory. Such Beings need not be "physical" in the sense that we know it.

The Seven Faces of God may be *facets* of a creature too advanced for anything our brains are capable of conceiving.

A thousand years before the birth of Christ, the Yogasutra listed the feats that advanced human beings were potentially capable of accomplishing:

- Making the body larger or smaller at will.
- Reaching all things, all places, the Moon or a distant planet.
- Making the will irresistible. (For example, diving into the earth as though it were water.)
- Mastering the production, disappearance, and transformation of things.
- Entering into another person's mind or body.
- Invisibility.

Such ideas do not come from the brains of mortal men but from a far greater source. In a multidimensional pluriverse, there may be many Godlike races capable of instantaneous teleportation and of "mastering the production, disappearance, and transformation" of anything—including the planets, the Sun, and our astoundingly complex biosphere.

The fact that God is Omniscient and Omnipotent is in total, violent conflict with the notion that humans (particularly scientists) are a collective form of God. The Supreme Creator of all the kingdoms, worlds, and galaxies of all the universes seems to have bestowed on each species the degree of freedom of choice befitting its purpose in the natural world.

Violation of this gift after repeated warnings (which Nature has provided when man has tampered with the environment, with recombinant DNA and nuclear fission) must inevitably bring erasure of that life form. To date, no one has satisfactorily explained the existence of the asteroid belt between Mars and Jupiter. It seems to be the remnants of a destroyed planet. Stars frequently explode and destroy their retinues of planets and all life in their systems. Astronomers and physicists claim to know why this happens and give perfectly logical-sounding reasons for such cataclysmic cosmic events.

But I think they do *not* know why such things occur.

ABOUT THE AUTHOR

Joseph Goodavage has written and published dozens of articles, for both scientific and general audience publications. Formerly with Chicago's City News Bureau, and reporter and writer for the NEW YORK DAILY NEWS syndicate, the CHICAGO TRIBUNE, and THE NEW YORK TIMES, Mr. Goodavage is a member of the American Society of Journalists and Authors, the New York Newspaper Guild, the American Federation of Astrologers, and the Authors Guild.

Mr. Goodavage has authored several books for NAL, including ASTROLOGY: THE SPACE AGE SCIENCE, WRITE YOUR OWN HOROSCOPE and, most recently, SEVEN BY SEVEN.

SIGNET Books of Related Interest

☐ **EIGHTH TOWER by John A. Keel.** Beams of light, voices from the heavens, the "little people," gods and devils, ghosts and monsters, and UFOs—spine-chilling but true case histories that reveal the shocking truth about our present position and future destiny in the cosmic scheme of things. (#E7460—$1.75)

☐ **ADVENTURES INTO THE PSYCHIC by Jess Stearn.** Startling, fully documented new evidence on the astonishing powers of the human mind. Whether you are a skeptic or a believer, this book will hold you spellbound.
(#W7822—$1.50)

☐ **THE POWER OF ALPHA THINKING: Miracle of the Mind by Jess Stearn.** Practice the positive meditation of Alpha and Biofeedback and reprogram your life. Complete with do-it-yourself exercises to Alpha. (#J7278—$1.95)

☐ **A TIME FOR ASTROLOGY by Jess Stearn.** The most complete book on the world of astrology illuminates the many amazing ways the stars can affect you and exactly what you can do about it. Illustrated with 30 charts and 5 tables. (#J7056—$1.95)

☐ **THE LOVERS' GUIDE TO SENSUOUS ASTROLOGY by Marlowe and Urna Gray.** How to meet, seduce and erotically please the playmate of your dreams. You'll discover more sensuous variations that you thought it was possible to know in a book that turns perfect strangers into ideal lovers—you'll wonder how you ever loved without it!
(#W7814—$1.75)

* Price slightly higher in Canada.

SIGNET Books from Martin Ebon

- [ ] **LOST SURVIVORS OF THE DELUGE by Gerd Von Hassler translated by Martin Ebon.** Riddles of the past are answered in a provocative study that presents indisputable evidence which proves that the prehistoric New World was "civilized" by Noah and his descendants after their own homeland was destroyed in the Flood.
 (#E8365—$1.75)*

- [ ] **THE SIGNET HANDBOOK OF PARA-PSYCHOLOGY edited by Martin Ebon.** The most comprehensive guide to the always fascinating and often astounding science of parapsychology, complete with the latest discoveries about out-of-the-body experiences, poltergeists, dreams and precognition, survival after death, mental telepathy and much, much more! (#J8406—$1.95)

- [ ] **REINCARNATION IN THE TWENTIETH CENTURY (revised) edited by Martin Ebon.** In this startling book about one of the most fascinating and controversial subjects of the century, a noted scholar has assembled the compelling testimony of those who claim to remember former lives. (#W8479—$1.50)*

- [ ] **THE AMAZING URI GELLER edited by Martin Ebon.** Is Uri Geller a psychic, the instrument of an alien intelligence seeking peaceful contact with Earth, or an adept fraud out to make his fame and fortune at the public's expense? The real story about the psychic of the century with eight pages of astonishing photos. (#W6475—$1.50)

- [ ] **MAHARISHI: The Founder of Transcendental Meditation edited by Martin Ebon.** A fascinating record of the phenomenal Hindu monk—his life, his work, his impact.
 (#W7012—$1.50)

 * Price slightly higher in Canada.

Big Bestsellers from SIGNET

- ☐ **SONG OF SOLOMON** by Toni Morrison. (#E8340—$2.50)*
- ☐ **MISTRESS OF OAKHURST** by Walter Reed Johnson. (#J8253—$1.95)
- ☐ **RIDE THE BLUE RIBAND** by Rosalind Laker. (#J8252—$1.95)*
- ☐ **KRAMER VS. KRAMER** by Avery Corman. (#E8282—$2.50)
- ☐ **RAPTURE'S MISTRESS** by Gimone Hall. (#E8422—$2.25)
- ☐ **GIFTS OF LOVE** by Charlotte Vale Allen. (#J8388—$1.95)
- ☐ **BELLADONNA** by Erica Lindley. (#J8387—$1.95)
- ☐ **THE GODFATHER** by Mario Puzo. (#E8508—$2.50)*
- ☐ **BLACK DAWN** by Christopher Nicole. (#E8342—$2.25)
- ☐ **NEVER CALL IT LOVE** by Veronica Jason. (#J8343—$1.95)*
- ☐ **TWINS** by Bari Wood and Jack Geasland. (#E8015—$2.50)
- ☐ **THE RULING PASSION** by Shaun Herron. (#E8042—$2.25)
- ☐ **CRAZY LOVE** by Phyllis Naylor. (#J8077—$1.95)
- ☐ **THE RAGING WINDS OF HEAVEN** by June Shiplett. (#J8213—$1.95)*
- ☐ **LEGEND** by Frank Sette. (#J8605—$1.95)*

* Price slightly higher in Canada.

THE NEW AMERICAN LIBRARY, INC.,
P.O. Box 999, Bergenfield, New Jersey 07621

Please send me the SIGNET BOOKS I have checked above. I am enclosing $_____ (please add 50¢ to this order to cover postage and handling). Send check or money order—no cash or C.O.D.'s. Prices and numbers are subject to change without notice.

Name _____

Address _____

City_____ State_____ Zip Code_____

Allow at least 4 weeks for delivery
This offer is subject to withdrawal without notice.